DESERT SHOWDOWN

It was hot and still. Far off, a dust devil danced among the Galleta grass and the creosote brush, but I saw no dust of human make. It could be I'd shaken them. Maybe we would have no trouble after all.

What made me turn my head I'll never know, but glancing over my left shoulder I caught just a glimpse of a rifle muzzle as somebody drew sight on me.

Mister, I left off of that rock like I was taking a free dive into a swimmin' hole, and I hit that heaped-up sand on my shoulder and rolled over. When I came up it was on one knee, the other leg stretched out ahead of me, and my Winchester coming up to firing position . . .

BENDIGO SHAFTER
BORDEN CHANTRY
BOWDRIE
BOWDRIE'S LAW
BRIONNE
THE BROKEN GUN
BUCKSKIN RUN
THE BURNING HILLS
THE CALIFORNIOS
CALLAGHEN
CATLOW
CHANCY
THE CHEROKEE TRAIL
COMSTOCK LODE
CONAGHER
CROSSFIRE TRAIL
DARK CANYON
DOWN THE LONG HILLS
THE EMPTY LAND
FAIR BLOWS THE WIND
FALLON
THE FERGUSON RIFLE
THE FIRST FAST DRAW
FLINT
FRONTIER
GUNS OF THE TIMBERLANDS
HANGING WOMAN CREEK
HELLER WITH A GUN
THE HIGH GRADERS
HIGH LONESOME
THE HILLS OF HOMICIDE
HONDO
HOW THE WEST WAS WON
THE IRON MARSHAL
THE KEY-LOCK MAN
KID RODELO
KILKENNY
KILLOE
KILRONE
KIOWA TRAIL
LAW OF THE DESERT BORN
THE LONESOME GODS
THE MAN CALLED NOON
THE MAN FROM SKIBBEREEN
MATAGORDA
MILO TALON
THE MOUNTAIN VALLEY WAR
NORTH TO THE RAILS
OVER ON THE DRY SIDE
THE PROVING TRAIL
THE QUICK AND THE DEAD

RADIGAN
REILLY'S LUCK
THE RIDER OF LOST CREEK
RIVERS WEST
THE SHADOW RIDERS
SHALAKO
SHOWDOWN AT YELLOW
  BUTTE
SILVER CANYON
SITKA
SON OF A WANTED MAN
THE STRONG SHALL LIVE
TAGGART
TO TAME A LAND
TUCKER
UNDER THE SWEET-
  WATER RIM
UTAH BLAINE
THE WALKING DRUM
WAR PARTY
WESTWARD THE TIDE
WHERE THE LONG GRASS
  BLOWS
YONDERING

Sackett Titles by
Louis L'Amour

1. SACKETT'S LAND
2. TO THE FAR BLUE
   MOUNTAINS
3. THE DAYBREAKERS
4. SACKETT
5. LANDO
6. MOJAVE CROSSING
7. THE SACKETT BRAND
8. THE LONELY MEN
9. TREASURE MOUNTAIN
10. MUSTANG MAN
11. GALLOWAY
12. THE SKY-LINERS
13. THE MAN FROM THE
    BROKEN HILLS
14. RIDE THE DARK TRAIL
15. THE WARRIOR'S PATH
16. LONELY ON THE
    MOUNTAIN
17. RIDE THE RIVER

Louis L'Amour
Mojave Crossing

BANTAM BOOKS
TORONTO • NEW YORK • LONDON • SYDNEY • AUCKLAND

MOJAVE CROSSING

A Bantam Book / January 1964

2nd printing .... August 1968	*4th printing ...... June 1970*
3rd printing .... August 1968	*5th printing .. September 1970*

New Bantam edition / April 1971

2nd printing ..... June 1971	*14th printing . December 1978*
3rd printing ... October 1971	*15th printing ... January 1979*
4th printing .. February 1972	*16th printing ... January 1979*
5th printing ..... July 1972	*17th printing ..... May 1979*
6th printing ... January 1973	*18th printing ..... May 1980*
7th printing ... August 1973	*19th printing ..... June 1980*
8th printing ..... July 1974	*20th printing .. February 1981*
9th printing . December 1974	*21st printing ... August 1981*
10th printing .. February 1976	*22nd printing ..... June 1982*
11th printing .. February 1977	*23rd printing ... March 1983*
12th printing . September 1977	*24th printing . December 1983*
13th printing ..... April 1978	*25th printing . September 1984*

26th printing ... December 1985

Photograph of Louis L'Amour
by John Hamilton—Globe Photos, Inc.

Library of Congress Catalog Card Number: 64-10937

All rights reserved.
Copyright © 1964 by Bantam Books, Inc.

This book may not be reproduced in whole or in part, by
mimeograph or any other means, without permission.
For information address: Bantam Books, Inc.

ISBN 0-553-25505-3

Published simultaneously in the United States and Canada

Bantam Books are published by Bantam Books, Inc. Its trade-
mark, consisting of the words "Bantam Books" and the por-
trayal of a rooster, is Registered in U.S. Patent and Trademark
Office and in other countries. Marca Registrada. Bantam
Books, Inc., 666 Fifth Avenue, New York, New York 10103.

PRINTED IN THE UNITED STATES OF AMERICA

H   35 34 33 32 31 30 29 28 27 26

to Parker

Mojave Crossing

one

When I saw that black-eyed woman a-looking at me I wished I had a Bible.

There I was, a big raw-boned mountain boy, rougher than a cob and standing six feet three inches in my socks, with hands and shoulders fit to wrassle mustang broncs or ornery steers, but no hand with womenfolks.

Nobody ever claimed that I was anything but a homely man, but it was me she was looking at in that special way she had.

Where we Sacketts come from in the high-up mountains of Tennessee, it is a known thing that if you sleep with a Bible under your pillow it will keep you safe from witches. Before they can do aught to harm you they must count every word in the Bible, and they just naturally can't finish that before daybreak, when they lose their power to hurt.

Yet when I taken a second look at that black-eyed, black-haired woman I thought maybe it was me should do the counting. She was medium tall, with a way about her that set a man to thinking thoughts best kept to himself. She had the clearest, creamiest skin you ever did see, and a mouth that fairly prickled the hair on the back of your neck.

Most of my years I'd spent shying around in the mountains or out on the prairie lands, with no chance to deal myself any high cards in society, but believe me, there's more snares in a woman's long lashes than in all the creek bottoms of Tennessee. Every time I taken my eyes from that black-haired witch woman it was in me to look back.

My right boot-toe was nudging the saddlebags at my feet, warning me I'd no call to take up with any woman, for there were thirty pounds of gold in those bags, not all of it mine.

The worst of it was, I figured things were already shaping for trouble. Three days hard-running I'd seen dust hanging over my back trail like maybe there was somebody back there who wanted to keep close to me without actually catching up. And that could only mean that trouble lay ahead.

Now, I'm no man who's a stranger to difficulty. No boy who walked out of Tennessee to fight for the Union was likely to be, to say nothing of all that had happened since. Seemed like trouble dogged my tracks wherever I put a foot down, and here was I, heading into strange country, running into a black-eyed woman.

She sat alone and ate alone, so obviously a lady that nobody made a move to approach her. This was a rough place in rough times, but a body would have thought she was setting up to table in Delmonico's or one of those fancy eastern places, her paying no mind to anything or anybody. Except, occasionally, me.

She wasn't all frills and fuss like a fancy woman, for she was dressed simple, but her clothes were made from rich goods. Everything about her warned me I'd best tuck in my tail and skedaddle out of there whilst I was able, for trouble doesn't abide only with fancy women. Even a good woman, with her ways and notions, can cause a man more trouble than he can shoot his way out of, and I'd an idea this here was no good woman.

Trouble was, there just was no place to run to.

Hardyville was little else but a saloon, a supply store, and a hotel at the crossing of the Colorado. Most of the year it was the head of navigation on the river, but there had been a time or two when steamboats had gone on up to the mines in Eldorado Canyon, or even to Callville.*

Come daybreak, I figured to cross the river on the first ferry and take out for the Bradshaw Road and Los Angeles, near the western ocean. It was talked among the Arizona towns that speculators out there would pay eighteen, maybe twenty dollars an ounce for gold, whilst in the mining camps a body could get but sixteen.

It was in my mind to sell my gold in Los Angeles, buy goods and mules, pack across the Mojave Desert and the Colorado, and sell my goods in the mining towns. With luck I'd show profit on my gold, and on my goods as well.

Nobody ever claimed I was any kind of a businessman, least of all me, but if a body can buy cheap and sell high he just naturally ain't liable to starve. Of course, in all things there was a reason, and in this case it was the difficulty of getting either gold or goods through a country full up with outlaws and Indians Whilst no businessman, I was pretty fair at getting from here to yonder, so I just bowed my neck and plunged in, figuring wherever a body could go a Smoky Mountain Sackett could go.

Speaking rightly, there were three kinds of Sack-

---

*Now under the waters of Lake Mead.

etts in Tennessee. The Smoky Mountain Sacketts, the Cumberland Gap Sacketts, and the Clinch Mountain Sacketts. These here last ones, they were a mean outfit and we had no truck with them unless at feuding time, when we were always pleased to have them on our side, for they were mean men in any kind of a shindig. But most of the time we held off from those Clinch Mountain boys.

There were some lowland Sacketts, too, living in the Cumberland Valley, but they were rich Sacketts and we paid them no mind. Pa, he always said we shouldn't hold it against them if they had money; chances were they couldn't he'p it, no ways.

All the Sacketts, even those no-account Sacketts from Clinch Mountain, run to boy-children. They had a saying over yonder that if you flung a stone into the brush you'd hit a Sackett boy, and likely, although it wasn't said, a Trelawney girl. I don't know what we Sackett boys would have done without the Trelawney girls.

But the only thing I was thinking of now was getting my old saddlebags across the Mojave and to Los Angeles, selling as well as I could, buying as cheap as possible, and getting back to the mines.

Now, when a beautiful woman or a handsome man receives attention it is taken as a matter of course; but I was a plain man, so when this black-eyed woman started paying me mind, I checked my hole card.

Not that I'd lacked for attention where women were concerned . . . not, at least, after they came to know me. Nor could it be said that I was downright distrustful of folks. There's a-plenty of just people in the world, but the flesh is weak and man is prone to sin . . . especially if a woman is involved.

But I was packing gold, and it came upon me to realize there is something about the presence of gold that is favorable to the breathing of beautiful women. And likely this woman, with her witch-black eyes, could see right through the leather of my saddlebags.

Only I'd been storing up pleasure for myself in thinking of a time when I could set up to table and eat a hot meal I hadn't fixed for myself, and sleep in a bed, if only for the strangeness of it. And if I high-tailed it out of here now I'd miss both.

For the life of me I couldn't imagine what a woman like this was doing in Hardyville. By the looks of her, she had come upriver on a steamboat, for her clothes showed no dust, as they would had she come by stage or wagon.

When the waitress brought my food the black-eyed woman stopped her, and asked, "Isn't it time for the stage for Los Angeles?"

"Have to get them a new stage," I said.

"What do you mean?"

"It ain't a-comin' in."

All of them were looking at me now, so I said, "Seen it back yonder." I was buttering a thick slab of bread. "He who was driving is dead . . . two holes alongside his spine. The stage is laying over in the canyon and the horses gone. Two other dead men . . . passengers."

"Are you sure?" This was Hardy asking.

"The buzzards were."

"You didn't go down to them?"

"Not for more'n a minute or two. No tellin' who was laying up in the rocks with a Winchester."

"Mojaves," somebody said, "or Hualapais."

"They wore moccasins, all right, but they weren't Indians. They were Comanche moccasins, and there's no Comanches out here."

Everybody started talking all to once and I set to eating, glad to be let alone. Anyway, it was likely I'd already talked too much. One of those men who'd done the shooting might be right here in this room, although I'd cast eyes about for moccasins when I first came in, habit-like. Seems to me a man has trouble enough in this world without borrowing more with careless words.

That black-eyed woman was talking to the waitress. "But if that stage has been wrecked, how long will it be before there's another?"

"Ma'am, you'll just have to abide. The next regular stage is Thursday."

This here was Monday, and I could see from that woman's face that she had to be shut of Hardyville long before that. And it wasn't just that this was a jumping-off place—she was scared.

That witch woman's lips turned pale and her black eyes grew large, like she'd seen a ghost. Maybe her own.

She turned sharp around to me and said, "Will you take me to Los Angeles with you?"

And me, like a damned fool, and without thinking, I said, "Yes."

It never does any good for a man to cuss himself, unless maybe it helps to impress on his mind what a fool he's been, but right then and there I did a fair to middling job of cussing myself out for seven kinds of a fool. Here I was, in a running hurry to get to Cailifornia—to Los Angeles, that is—and I'd burdened myself with a woman. And by the look of her she'd need coddling.

Well, I'd been fool enough for one day, and maybe I could get out of this yet. "You'll need horses," I said. "Are you packing much gear?"

"My trunk can come by stage. All I'll need will be the two carpetbags."

"My pack horse can handle them if they aren't heavy," I said, "but you'll need two ridin' horses. This here's a fast trip I'm makin'."

"Thank you," she said. "If you will get them for me, I'll pay you in Los Angeles. All I have"—she smiled beautifully—"is my stage ticket and a bank draft too large to cash here."

"I—" I started to object that I didn't have the money, but those saddlebags were pushing at my toe and I'd a sneaking feeling—with no reason for it that I could make sense out of—that she knew what was in those bags.

"All right," I said, and lost my last chance to back out of it.

No getting around it, I was upset. It was my notion to make a fast trip to Los Angeles, which was my reason for two horses, switching from one to the other. Now I had that woman to care for, and no telling what she was like on a horse.

Taking another fill of coffee from the pot on the table, I happened to look across at the bar. A man standing there was looking my way and listening to two others. There seemed to be something familiar about the biggest of them. He was a man as tall as I was, and some heavier. He was a dark, strong-looking man who wore a gun like a man who could use it. His back was to me, and he had a fine set of shoulders on him . . . he was built like a man who could punch.

That woman hadn't moved, and our tables were only two feet apart. Best thing was to get it settled right off.

"If you ride with me," I said, and I'm afraid my tone was kind of rough, "you will be ready to go, come daybreak . . . and that doesn't mean sun-up. It means the first gray in the sky."

Shoving back my chair, I got up. "Can you use a gun?"

Well, sir, she surprised me. "Yes," she said, "I can handle a rifle." And then she smiled at me, and

7

you've never seen such a smile. "And please do not disturb yourself. I shall be no trouble to you."

Fishing those saddlebags off the floor with my left hand, I stood up, dropping a quarter on the table for my meal. Then I taken up my Winchester with my right hand and walked to the door.

A voice spoke behind me, and I had a feeling the big man had turned to look, and I knew that voice was an invitation to turn around, an invitation to trouble. Stepping outside, I closed the door behind me and stood alone in the soft desert night.

It was very still. The Colorado River rustled by out there in the darkness, and beyond the river loomed the Dead Mountains. Over there a narrow point of Nevada came down to join borders with California.

Uneasily, I looked westward into those miles of desert, and the hunch rode my shoulders that I'd see blood and grief before those miles were behind me. A fool I was to entangle myself with that black-eyed woman.

Of a sudden I realized the thing I'd ought to do was to leave now. True, the ferry was not operating, but swimming the river at this point was no new thing. Beale had done it with his camels, and fine swimmers they proved to be.

There was a light in the window of Hardy's cabin. Crossing to it, I tapped on the door, not too loud.

Being a wise man, he spoke before opening the door, but when I told I wanted to make a dicker on some horses, he opened up, but he held a pistol in his hand, which surprised me none at all.

"Yes," he replied, when I had explained myself. "I've two good horses, but they'll cost you."

He slid his gun into its holster and picked up his coat. He started to put it on, then stopped and looked over at me. "Are you taking that Robiseau woman out of here?"

"I never asked her name, nor she mine. She wishes to go to Los Angeles, and I'm riding that way."

He shrugged into his coat. "You're borrowing trouble. Look, I don't know you. You just drifted in here out of nowhere, but that woman is running from something, and whatever it is or whoever it is will bundle you into her package. I mean, they'll resent interference."

"Whatever it is," I said, "she's a woman alone, and needs help."

He didn't say any more, but led the way to the stable and lighted a lantern. The horses in their stalls rolled their eyes at me. There were only a few stalls, for his own good stock. The mustang stuff was in the corrals out back.

One of the two horses he showed me was a liver-colored stallion with a white nose and three white stockings; a long-barreled animal built for speed and staying power, and one of the finest-looking horses I'd seen, and big for this country. It would weigh a good thousand pounds and maybe a mite over. The other horse was a short-coupled gelding, mouse-colored, with a fine head and powerful hindquarters. It was somewhat smaller than the other, but all horse.

We dickered there by lantern light, but he knew I had to have those horses, and he got his price. Yet high as they came, they were worth every penny of it. He had bought them from an Army officer who was changing station. The horses had been the officer's private mounts, and the smaller one had been broken for a woman to ride.

"You made a good buy," Hardy acknowledged,

"although I got my price. There's no better horses around, unless it's those you've got."

We stood in the stable door, listening to the river. "She came up on the boat," Hardy volunteered, "and just missed the stage to Prescott."

"Prescott?"

"Uh-huh. Then she changed her mind and decided on Los Angeles. Seems to me like she wants the first stage out, no matter where it goes."

He paused and we stood there in silence, with me thinking about that road west, and those men who had been following me.

There'd been a time, back along the trail, when I was not sure . . . maybe they were just traveling the same way . . . but when I left Beale's Springs I headed up to the Coyote Wells and got in there with time to spare. Those riders never showed up, although I'd seen their dust on my trail. That could mean only one thing—they were lying out in the hills, making dry camp, just so's I wouldn't see them.

Short of midnight I had left my fire burning low, saddled up, and taken off across the hills. My trail led west, toward Union Pass; but I got a notion, and after whipsawing back and forth in the trail, I cut off through the brush toward the south. South, then west, and through Secret Pass.

At Secret Spring I made camp and slept until well past daybreak. Then, after saddling up, I had climbed to the top of the cliff and looked off to the east and north. Sure enough, there was dust and movement on my back trail. Through my field glasses—taken off a dead Confederate officer on the battlefield—I could just make out four riders.

They had ridden on by the place where I'd turned off, discovering too late that I'd cut out somewhere. Now they were scouting their back trail to find the turn-off. They were a good ten, twelve miles off and in the bottom of Sacramento Wash.

Descending to my outfit, I had mounted up and followed the Secret Pass trail into Hardyville.

Nobody had ridden in, so they were lying out again, fearful of being seen by me, which might mean that I knew them and they feared recognition.

"Whoever it is," Hardy said now, "who wants that Robiseau woman, he wants her pretty bad, and wants her himself."

There was meaning in the way he said it, and I turned to look at him. "Keep out of it, friend," Hardy went on. "Three of those men in the saloon are watching her for somebody, and they shape up like grief a-plenty for anybody in their way."

"I gave her my word."

"Your funeral."

"Maybe," I said gloomily. "I'm not a trouble-hunting man. Not a one of us Sacketts ever was."

Hardy gave a quick, funny sort of sound. "Did you say *Sackett*? Is your name *Sackett*?"

"Sure . . . do you know the name?"

He turned away from me. "Get out . . . get out while you can."

He started off, walking very fast, but when he had taken but a couple of steps he turned around. "Does she know your name? Have you told her that?"

"No . . . no, I never did, come to think on it."

"Of course not . . . of course." He looked at me, but I could not see the expression in his eyes. There was only light enough to see his face under the brim of his hat. "Take my advice and don't tell her . . . not, at least, until you reach Los Angeles—if you do."

He walked away, leaving me almighty puzzled, but convinced the time to leave was now.

two

When I looked into the window of the saloon the
men at the bar were still drinking their liquor and
talking it up. The black-eyed woman was gone.

The hotel had only four special rooms and I had
latched onto one of those. The only other occupied
one was the one given to the Robiseau girl, so I
slipped in the back door and went to her room and
tapped ever so gently.

There was a quick rustle of clothing inside, and
something that sounded like a click of a drawed-
back gun-hammer, and then her voice, low. "I have
a pistol. Go away."

"Ma'am," I whispered right back to her, "you want
to go to Los Angeles, you come to this door, an'
quick."

She came, easing it open a crack. The pistol looking through the opening was no feisty little-girl
pistol. It was a sure enough he-coon of a pistol, a .44
Navy Colt.

"Ma'am, if you want to get to Los Angeles, you get
dressed. We're leaving out of here in twenty
minutes."

13

I'll give her this—she didn't say aye, yes, or no, she just lowered that gun muzzle and said, "I'll be ready. At the stable?"

"The ferry," I said, "only we're going to swim it. The ferry stopped crossing at sundown."

I'd never left hold of my gold. nor my rifle, but I stepped across the hall and picked up the rest of my gear, took one longing look at that bed, and then tiptoed down the hall and out to the stable.

When I made my dicker for the horses I'd gotten an old saddle thrown in, and now I saddled up two horses.

We'd be riding those two, and leading two spare saddle horses and my pack horse By swapping horses, we could make faster time than most anybody coming after us, and I was figuring on that.

But that wasn't the only bee I had in my bonnet. True it was that I'd never ridden those westward trails that lay before us, but I'd listened to a sight of talk about them from those who had. and it came over me that a body might strike off on a new route and make it through, if he was lucky.

That would be something to keep in mind.

She was at the river, carpetbags and all, when I got there with the horses. She had dressed in an all-fired hurry, but she didn't show it. Helping her into the saddle, I got the feel of her arm. and she was all woman, that one. She swung up, hooking one knee around the horn like she was riding a sidesaddle, and we taken off.

The water was dark, and there was more current than a body would expect. Walking our horses into the water, I pointed across. "Make for that peak, and when you get over there, don't call out. If we get separated, just stay put. I'll find you."

Holding my rifle and gunbelt high, I rode on into the water, and she followed.

I felt the stallion's feet go out from under him as he hit deep water.

He was a strong swimmer, and when I glanced back I saw that woman right behind me, her horse swimming strong too. We made it up the bank, and as I turned to glance back I heard a door slam and somebody shouted and swore.

"What the hell?" I said. "They ain't found out a-ready?"

She pulled up beside me. "Maybe the ferryman told them," she said.

"*Ferryman?* How would he know?"

She turned and looked at me like I was a fool. "Why, I asked him to take us across. He refused."

Me, I'd never hit a woman, but I wanted to right then. I wanted to hit her the worst way. Instead, I just turned my horse and started off into the Dead Mountains, mad enough to tackle a grizzly with my bare hands.

"Ma'am," I said roughly, "you played hell. The reason we started now was to get some distance between us before daylight. Now you've tipped them off and they will be comin' right behind us."

"But they couldn't!" she protested. "He's not—I mean, why would anybody want to catch us?"

"You know that better than me, but even Hardy knew some of those men back at the saloon were there to watch you. He told me so."

She shut up then, having nothing more to say and no chance to say it, for I led off, walking that stallion fast. Having the fresh horse was going to spell my two horses, and they could use the rest.

The trail lay white under the hoofs of the horses; the desert night was still. That liver-colored stallion went out of there like he had a fire under his tail, and I'll hand it to that black-eyed girl. No matter how she had to sit her saddle, she stayed with me.

No telling what those men wanted with her, but in these times there were white men with bloodier hands than any Indian, and I was asking for no trouble I could avoid with honor. Just short of daylight I drew up and we swapped saddles to fresh horses, but it was an hour later before I made my move.

The Dead Mountains lay behind us and I turned up a dry wash. If my memory was working along the lines of what I'd been told, this was Piute Wash and it ran due north for quite a spell, then a dim trail would cut over toward Piute Spring.

There was no time for talk, and I had no mind for it, wanting only to put distance between myself and those men back there. They might run us down, or they might wait until the steamboat came in with whoever was on it.

At Piute Spring, on the eastern foot of the range, we pulled up long enough to water the horses and drink a mite ourselves. The valley ahead of us was mostly flat-seeming land covered with Joshua trees. We went out of the shadow of the Piute Range and into the Joshuas, and at first they were scattered, then they thickened up. Once into the Joshuas, we slowed down to raise as little dust as possible.

There were thousands of those trees there in the valley and they offered a might of cover. From a height somebody might have picked us out, but nobody on our own level was likely to, so we pushed on, holding parallel to the old Government Road from Fort Mojave.

The sun had gone before we sighted the draw I was looking for and, riding up a hundred yards, came to Rock Spring. There was little water, which suited me, for when we left I didn't mean for there to be any.

The Robiseau woman looked pale and drawn when

I reached up to take her by the waist to swing her down. Tired as she was, she wasn't ready to haul down her flag. As her feet touched the ground she let her hands rest on my forearms and said, "You're very strong."

"I'd better be."

She gave me an odd look, but I turned away and began gathering sticks for a fire. The spot was sheltered, and there was time for coffee and a quick meal.

This was something I'd done so often that it was no trick at all, and by the time I'd stripped the saddles the water was boiling and the food about ready.

"You haven't told me your name."

"Folks call me Tell."

"Only that?"

"It's enough."

"I am Dorinda Robiseau."

It sounded like a made-up name, but I'd known folks with real names that sounded made up. "Pleased to meet you."

"You haven't asked me why I couldn't wait for the stage."

"Your business."

She acted like she wanted to explain, but I had no plan to get more involved than I was. I'd been fool enough to take her along, but the sooner I got shut of her the better.

Sitting under the stars, we ate a quick meal, then finished the coffee I'd made. "There's something about a campfire . . ." she said. "I like to look into the coals."

"Take your last look," I said. "I'm putting it out." When I'd kicked sand over the coals I added, "Fool thing, looking into a fire. When you look away you're blind . . . and men have been killed that-away."

I saddled up and loaded our packs. She looked like she couldn't believe what I was doing, but I said, "If you're coming with me, get up in the saddle."

"You're going on? *Tonight?*"

"You want your friends to catch us? You can bet if I knew where this spring was, they'll know. In the desert a man's travelin' is pretty well cut and dried by where he can find water."

Whoever those men were, they must be wanting her pretty bad to follow us as they were. Of course, there was a chance they were following *me*. They might be the same outfit that had trailed me to Hardyville. There'd been a bunch of renegades drifting through the country raiding ranches or mine prospects for supplies. Somebody said they were a Frisco outfit that had come down through Nevada.

As for this Robiseau girl, she might be somebody's wife, or she might have been involved in some shady doings out California way. Anyway, they needed her bad enough to chase her.

Meanwhile, I'd been doing some pondering of the situation, and there was nothing about it to make a man content. According to what I'd been told when preparing to start westward, it was twenty miles to the next water at Marl Spring, almost due west of where we were now. Most of that twenty miles lay out on bare desert, and if we started from here now we could make it by daylight—if we didn't stray from the trail.

If we strayed . . . Well, there were bones a-plenty out there on the desert to answer that question. Moreover, I had me a tired woman, in no shape for such a ride.

In those days every saloon was a clearing house for information. Sitting around in a saloon or stand-

ing at a bar, loafing in a cow camp or riding the
trail, men just naturally talked about places they'd
been. It was likely to be all a body would ever get
to know about trails or towns until he traveled
them, so men listened and remembered.

Nobody reckoned in miles. Not often, at least.
Distance was reckoned in time, and a place was a
day's ride, or two days' ride, or whatever.

And many a cowhand who had never left Texas
could describe in detail the looks of Hickok, Earp,
Tilghman, Masterson, or Mathers. If a body wasn't
able to recognize the town marshal he'd best not try
to cut any fancy didoes in western towns.

So I knew a good bit about the Mojave, although
I'd not crossed it before. I knew what landmarks
to look for, and the trouble to expect. Only nobody
had told me I'd be crossing the wide sand with a
fine-dressed woman behind me.

Well, it was twenty miles to water if I held to the
trail, but there was water south along the Providence
Mountains, and if we could locate one of those
springs we could hole up for the night, then work
our way south. We'd be taking big risks, venturing
off into the desert thataway, but there was a good
chance we'd leave all pursuit behind.

And so it was that when we left out of Rock
Spring, we headed south.

The night, as desert nights are inclined to be, was
cool . . . almost cold. There were many stars, and
around us lifted the jagged shoulders of black,
somber-looking mountains. We went at an easy
pace, the ground being rough and the country un-
familiar, and we had to pick our way. So it was
over an hour of riding before we covered the six
miles to Black Canyon.

There was a spring in the canyon, but we took no
time to look for it, pushing on toward the south.

Getting through the canyon, which was close to impassable, was a struggle. By daylight it might have been no trouble, but at night it used up time, and by the time we covered the four additional miles to Granite Well, we were tuckered.

We made dry camp a short way from the well, bedding down on a patch of drift sand among the rocks. Rolling out my bed, I pointed at it. "You roll up there. I'll sleep on the sand."

"I've no right to take your bed."

"Don't argue," I said shortly. "I can't have you falling out of the saddle tomorrow, and what we did today will look like one of your pink tea parties to what we got ahead of us."

It was rugged, broken country, mostly rock and drift sand, with some low-growing desert brush, and I lay awake for some time, speculating on our chances of getting through. Mostly, folks went by the northern route, following the old Government Road or Spanish Trail across the desert and over Cajon Pass. But with men following us with no good intent, it seemed best to risk the run to the south.

There was another pass down thataway, or so Joe Walker had told me. The Indians had used it a time or two, and some Spanish man had gone through the pass fifty or sixty years before. It was a risky trip, but we Sacketts always had an urge to try new country, and the time was right. As for that black-eyed woman . . . she should see some new country, too. Although I wasn't sure she was going to take to it.

A time or two I glanced over at Dorinda Robiseau. She lay quiet, resting easy, as she should have, for that bed of mine was a good one, and the sand I'd spread it on was deep and free of rocks, more comfortable than many a mattress. I could only see the white of her face, the darkness of her loosened hair.

She would be a trial in the days to come, but somehow I felt better just having her there.

It worried me, though . . . why were those men chasing her? And were they the law?

Remembering the men at the bar, I doubted it. They had a bad look about them. One thing was sure: if we faced up to each other out here in this lonely desert I was going to be glad that I was packing a gun.

That big-shouldered man who had stood with his back to me . . . he worried me. Why was there something familiar about him?

I awakened with a start, coming from a sound sleep to sharp attention.

Dorinda was sitting up, wide-eyed. "I heard something," she whispered.

"What?"

"I don't know. Something woke me."

My six-shooter was in my hand, and I looked first at the horses. They were standing heads up, looking off across the desert toward the east.

Rolling up, I put my six-shooter down carefully and shook out my boots—scorpions take notions to hide in boots and such like—and tugged them on.

A glance at the stars told me it was shaping up for daybreak. "Get up, and be very quiet," I said. "We're moving out."

She offered me no argument, and I'll give her this: she made herself ready in quicker time than I'd expected from any tenderfoot woman. By the time I'd saddled fresh horses, she had my bed rolled, and rolled good and tight.

Standing close in the dark, I said, "There's another spring not more than a mile over to the east. Sound carries far through a desert night."

Me, I wasn't altogether sure that whoever had made that sound was that far away, but it could be somebody searching for a waterhole.

We stepped into our saddles and I led off, heading due south, and keeping our horses in soft sand wherever I could. The Providence Mountains loomed high on our right, bleak, hard-shouldered mountains.

It was rugged going, but the night was cool and there was enough gray in the sky to enable a man to pick his trail. After riding about eight miles we left the rocks behind and had the Providence Mountains still on our right, with bald and open desert on our left, stretching away for miles toward distant hills.

"We're riding south," she said.

It was a question more than a statement, so I gave her the answer. "You want to get to Los Angeles, don't you? Well, I'm leaving the trail to them. We're going south, and then west through another pass."

What I didn't tell her was that I had only heard of that pass, and had only a rough idea of where it was. I knew that a stage line and a freight road went through that pass to the placer diggings around La Paz, on the Colorado.

The sky turned to lemon over the distant mountains, a warning that the sun would soon be burning over us. Somewhere to the south there were other springs, but I doubted if they would be easily found. The desert has a way of hiding its water in unexpected places, sometimes marked by willows, cottonwood, or palm trees, but often enough right out in a bottom with nothing but low brush around, and not a likely thing to indicate water. And we wouldn't have time to spend looking.

She rode up alongside me. "You're not a very talkative man."

"No, ma'am."

"Are you married?"

"If you're wonderin' about that scar on my cheek-bone, I got that in a knife fight in New Orleans."

"You have no family?"

"Me? I got more family than you could shake a stick at. I got family all over the country . . . only I am a lonesome kind of man, given to travel and such. I never was one to abide."

She looked at me curiously and, it seemed to me, kind of sharp. Then she said, "Where are you from, Mr. Tell? You hadn't said."

"No, ma'am. I hadn't."

We rode on for a couple of miles after that. A road runner showed up and raced out ahead of us, seeming glad of the company. Overhead there was nothing but sky, a sky changing from gray to brass with the sun coming up. Those mountains on our right, they were cool now, but within two hours they'd be blasting heat back at us.

"A few miles now, you keep your eyes open. We'll come up to a water hole, and I'd prefer not to miss it."

She offered no comment, and it was just as well. But she was a mighty pretty woman, and I'd have preferred riding easy with her, not worrying about folks coming up on me unexpected.

"You in some kind of trouble, ma'am?"

"I hadn't mentioned it," she said, coolly enough.

Well, that was fair. Only I was taking a risk, helping her this way.

It grew hot . . . and hotter. Not a breath of air stirred. The white sands around us turned to fire.

Heat waves shimmered a veil across the distance. We saw strange pools of water out there on the desert. Sweat trickled into our eyes. Our horses plodded along slowly; sweat streaked the gray film

23

of dust that lay over them, and over us. Neither of us was of any mind to talk now.

From time to time I turned to look back, for we were out in the open, masked only by the shimmering heat waves and the wall of the mountain along which we rode. There was nothing behind us but heat waves and the far-off shoulder of mountain.

Cook's Well was some place along here, but we missed it, and I was of no mind to waste time in search. Blind Spring lay somewhere ahead, and if we missed that, there would be no water until Cottonwood, down at the end of the mountain chain.

Had they cut in after us? Or were they, as I hoped, riding west along the Government Road toward Marl Spring?

"It might make a lot of difference," I spoke out suddenly, "if I knew how anxious they were to find you."

She let her horse go on a few steps before she made answer, and then she said, "The man who is after me would kill you or a half dozen others to put his hands on me . . . and then he would kill me."

Well, that answered that.

At high noon we drew up and I helped her down. I switched saddles and sponged out the mouths of our horses with water from a canteen. We each had a drink, and then we mounted up again and started on.

All the long day through we pushed on, and it was coming on to dark when I finally gave up on Blind Spring. We'd been too far out from the mountain or too close in, one or the other. The water in our canteens was low, and I hated to think what would happen if we didn't find water soon. We might make it, but the horses could not; and without the horses we would be helpless.

At dusk we halted and stripped the saddles from

our horses and I worked over them, rubbing them down, sponging out their mouths. Whatever Dorinda thought she wasn't inclined to say, nor was I inclined to listen.

The night came on, soft and dark, with the stars hanging easy in the sky. A cool wind blew up from somewhere, just a smidgin of it, but it felt good.

When I was finished with the horses I dug into my saddlebags for the last of the bread. It was hard and dry, but when I broke off a chunk and passed it to her, she tied into it like it was cake. We sat there on a sandbank, chewing away, and finally she said, "We're in trouble, aren't we?"

"It's like this," I said. "According to what I was told, from the point of the mountain we've got a three-cornered chance. Within three or four miles of this place there are three springs, they say, so we've a fair chance of locating one of them."

There was little time for rest, but trusting to the horses to warn us of any trouble coming, she rolled up in my bed and I hunkered down in the sand, working out a hollow for my body that came up on both sides of me, and there we rested.

In the morning, when I was pulling on my boots in the light of the last lone star, I saw Dorinda was awake, lying quiet, looking up at the star. "This country," I commented, "is hell on women and horses."

She did not turn her head or reply for several minutes, and then when I stood up to sling my gunbelt around my hips she said, "You get me to Los Angeles . . . that's all I ask."

I didn't answer her. With my bandana I carefully wipped the dust from the action of my pistol, checking the roll of the cylinder. She was asking a whole lot more than she knew, and right there I figured not to make any promises I couldn't keep.

25

When we had saddled up I said to her, "Just let the bridle alone. From here on, our horses might find water quicker by themselves."

Though I'd been told that Cottonwood was over the toe of the mountain from where we were, I decided to chance the other two springs figuring there was no use wasting time in perhaps the wrong direction. So I headed south and let that stallion have his head.

For a while he plodded on, seeming uninterested in much of anything, but then a change in the wind brought his head up and he quickened his step, bearing off to the right toward what I guessed would be the Old Dad Mountains. But as we drew closer I could see there were two small ranges with a break between them.

In a little cove in the rocks we found a spring. There was a small trickle of water, and we let the horses drink their fill. After filling our canteens, we started on.

A dozen miles further along we found Willow Spring, with a good flow of water and some willows and a few cottonwoods around, most of them no bigger than whipstocks. Leaving Dorinda to freshen up, I took up my Winchester and hiked it to the crest of the ridge, where I could look over our back trail.

There was a flat rock that lay half in shadow, and down in front of it, about six to eight feet lower, a patch of white drift sand. Sitting on the edge of the rock where the shadow had cooled it off a mite, I studied our back trail toward the end of the Providence Range.

It was hot and still. Far off over the desert a dust devil danced among the Galleta grass and the creosote brush, but I saw no dust of human make. It could be we had shaken them. Maybe we would have no trouble after all.

What made me turn my head I'll never know, but glancing over my left shoulder I caught just a glimpse of a rifle muzzle as somebody drew sight on me.

Mister, I left off of that rock like I was taking a free dive into a swimmin' hole, and I hit that heaped-up sand on my shoulder and rolled over. When I came up it was on one knee, the other leg stretched out ahead of me, and my Winchester coming up to firing position.

The echo of at least two shots hung in the hot desert afternoon. I saw a man come around a rock and I tightened my finger on that trigger and made the dust jump on his jacket.

It was no great shooting, for he was no more than thirty yards off. I'd no idea where he'd come from, but one thing I did know. He wasn't going any place else. That .44 ca'tridge bought him a free ticket to wherever the good Lord intended, and I up and scooted down among those rocks, a-duckin' and a-dodgin' and a-squirmin' among rocks and brush, my shoulders braced for a bullet that never came.

When I hit the brush I was runnin' all out, and the next thing I know there's a squeal of startled irritation and there's that black-eyed woman holding her dress in front of her and starin' at me so fierce I had a notion to go back and face those guns. But I had another notion that beat that one altogether.

"Lady," I said, "unless you want to ride out of here naked, you'd better dress faster'n you ever did. They've come upon us."

A bullet spat sand over my boots and I rolled over in the brush and laid all flat out, peeking through the willow leaves for something to throw lead at. I saw nothing.

The echoes died away, and the afternoon was hot and still as ever. I'd no idea who was out there, or how many, but when they'd started shootin' at me they opened the ball, and I was going to call a few tunes my own self.

After a moment I eased back into the willows and went for the horses. They were out of sight among the rocks, and when I got to them I stood by, waiting for that woman to come up. While I waited I kept a sharp eye out for trouble and kept thinking about that range of hills to the south . . . all of four miles away, and all of it bald desert.

Nobody needed to tell me that whatever we did, we'd have to clear out of here. There was too much cover around from which these springs could be taken under fire. When that witch woman came out of the brush, her black eyes sparking fire, I didn't wait for any fancy talk. I just taken her up by the waist and threw her into the saddle and said, "Ride, lady!" And I went up into my saddle and we taken out of there like hell a-chasin' tanbark.

Somebody started shootin', and I caught time for one quick glance over my shoulder and saw there were four or five anyway, and then two more came up out of the ground right ahead of me. I shot into the chest of the first one, firing my Winchester one-handed, like you'd hold a pistol The other one let fly at me and damned near busted my eardrums, and then my horse went into him. I heard him scream when a hoof smashed into his chest, but I only had time to hope that hoof wouldn't get hung up on the ribs.

Swinging wide to get that woman and the other horses ahead of me, I levered three fast shots back at those men, but I didn't hit anything but desert and rock. Ricochets have a nasty whine, though, and I caught a picture of the men duckin' for cover . . . and then all they could see of us was our dust.

We had good horses, and those men in tryin' to

sneak up on us had left theirs somewhere behind them. We were runnin' all out and reachin' for the shadow of the Bristol Mountains before I looked back and saw them come out of the hills, far back.

Closing in beside the Robiseau woman, I said, "Next time you take a bath it better be in Los Angeles."

three

It worried me that those men had come up on me from out of nowhere. Somebody in the lot of them was a tracker, or a shrewd one at judging what a man had in mind, and it left me uncertain of what to do. Having a woman with me complicated matters . . . or would if I let it.

Whatever they'd had in mind to start off with, it was a shooting matter now. There were three men down, and it was likely all three were dead, or hurting something fierce, and it wasn't likely the others would pull off and forget it.

Until now I'd been lucky—unlucky that they found us at all, but lucky in that I got off scot-free and didn't catch lead myself. Nor the woman or horses.

There was only one thing I could see to do, and that was to make them so miserable trying to catch us that they'd quit . . . if they had quit in them, which I doubted. So far it had cost them, but it was up to me to make it cost them more.

We crossed over the Bristol Mountains and headed due south for a pass in the Sheep Holes, thirty-five or forty miles off, with not a drop of water anywhere between.

On the horizon, not far ahead of us, loomed the black cone of a volcanic crater, and the black of a lava field. Beyond lay a wide dry lake, and I pointed our horses right at the spot where lava and dry lake joined, and we rode on.

After a while, when we looked back, the notch in the mountains through which we had come was gone, vanished behind a shoulder of the mountain. There was no sound, there was no movement but our own, and the tiny puffs of white dust that lifted from the face of the *playa* as our horses walked.

Behind us were shimmering heat waves, before us and around us the air wavered, and changed the looks of things. Small rocks seemed to tower above the desert, and the sparse brush seemed to be trees. Sweat streaked the flanks of our horses, dust rose around us. We were in a lost world, shut out from all about us by distance and by the shimmering heat.

Far off, something more than twenty miles away, loomed a blue range of hills . . . the Sheep Hole Mountains. Beyond them would be more desert and more mountains.

Would they follow us? Or, wiser than we were, mightn't they turn and ride right to Los Angeles, knowing we would come there?

Only, of course, they did not know. We might go to San Diego, or we might ride back north and go to San Francisco along the coast road.

They had to follow, and before they caught up with us I figured to lead them a chase. If they wanted tracks to follow, I aimed to show them a-plenty, and across some wild country. Only thing was, this black-eyed woman wasn't going to like it. In fact, I figured she regretted her bargain already. What waited her when those men caught up with us, I couldn't say, but it would have to be almighty bad to equal what lay ahead of us now.

Joe Walker and Old Bill Williams, mountain men both of them, had told me a good deal about the Mojave, but I'd learned of it from others as well, including a couple of Hualapai Indians I'd met in Prescott, both of whom had raided the ranchos for horses. It had been these Indians who told me most of what I knew of San Gorgonio Pass.

Desert travel was not new to me, for I'd crossed the cap rock of west Texas by the Goodnight-Loving Trail, and I'd been across the White Sands of New Mexico, as well as made a trip up the *Jornada del Muerto*, the "journey of death," so I was no tenderfoot when it came to deserts.

The desert can be a friendly place to a man on the dodge, but it is always better to hole up some place and wait for sundown. We were doing the worst thing a body could do in traveling by day, under a hot sun. The trouble was, those men back there behind us weren't about to give us any time.

Nobody knew better than me how lucky I'd been in that shindig back there, and it wasn't likely to happen that way again.

We pushed on, sagging in the saddle, the horses plodding steadily. Only me, I taken a look, time to time, to see if anything was gaining on us. Twice we stopped and I sponged out the horses' mouths and gave that Dorinda girl a mouthful of water to drink.

At sundown we could see mountains close ahead of us, and I began searching for the pass. One long arm of mountain had showed up to the east of us, and soon there was another on our right. A notch showed itself and I headed for that, glancing back one last time. There was a thin trail of something that might be dust, hanging against the sky.

In the cool dark, with a kit fox yapping somewhere up in the rocks, we rode through the Sheep Hole Mountains and made dry camp in a tiny cove.

Me, I was dead beat, and when I took that black-eyed Dorinda from her horse she could scarce stand, so I helped her to a place on the sand and kindled ourselves a hatful of fire and made coffee. Nobody needed to tell me how much she needed a hot drink, and I wasn't against the idea myself. Meanwhile, I checked out my Winchester, then my pistol. Rummaging around in my bedroll, I dug out a spare Colt, and made sure it was loaded, too.

"You killed a man back there," she said suddenly.

"Yes, ma'am. Maybe two or three."

"You don't seem bothered by it."

"They were comin' at me."

I poured out a cup of coffee for her and sat back on my heels, far enough from the fire not to be easily seen, and far enough from the crackle of the flames to hear if anything came upon us.

"I never had it in mind to shoot at any man, ma'am, but when somebody takes up a gun and comes for you in anger, he borrows grief. He was fetching trouble, so I gave him what he asked for."

She was half asleep already, and I passed her over a piece of jerked beef to chew on. "Go ahead," I told her, "it doesn't look like much, but there's a lot of stayin' quality in it."

After chewing a while myself, I said, "Carryin' a gun is a chancy thing. Sooner or later a man is put in position to use it. And a body has to figure that if somebody packs iron he plans to use it when the time comes; and if he draws it out, he plans to shoot."

I saw that she was fast asleep, so I covered her with a blanket and killed the fire. Then I went out and rubbed my horses down and gave them water, just a mite squeezed into their mouths. It wasn't much, and they wished for more; but it was all I had to offer, and it's likely they understood.

Taking my Winchester, I prowled around, and stood off under the stars, listening. This was spooky country, with big Joshua trees hither and yon, any one of which might be a man standing there. But the desert night was cool, and mean-tired though I was, it felt likely to my spirit.

Work and war never gave me much time for poetry, but there was a man in my outfit during the fighting near Shiloh who fancied it, and a time or two he'd quoted things at me from a book he carried in his shirt. I thought of it now, wishing I had some of those words he used to speak of the desert night.

Sitting down on a rock, I sort of listened and waited, studying the night with my ears, and each sound held meaning for me. Sometimes I had to sort the sounds a mite, but I knew what each one was . . . and I heard no sound of man nor horse, no creak of saddle, clink of metal, or brush of garment upon stone.

That woman back there was done in. Like it or not, we had to hole up somewhere and give her time to rest, but the worst of it was, one of those men in that outfit trailing us was a tracker and a hunter, and a sight better than most. It was that man who worried me, for if he continued to be as good as he'd been so far, we would be facing a showdown a lot sooner than I hoped.

More and more I wondered what I'd got myself into, and what Dorinda Robiseau had done to make them want her so much.

Not that she wasn't a beautiful woman, and the kind of woman any man would want. Even now, tired out as she was, she was lovely. But there was more to it than that. And the chances were good that I'd gotten myself on the wrong side of the law. Still, none of those men back at Hardyville had been wearing a badge . . . nor did they look likely to. Though all the men who wore badges through the western lands could not be said to measure up to a proper standard.

After a while I went back to our corner, checked the horses again, and burrowed into the sand to sleep.

But sleep did not come, dead tired though I was, for it came upon me that I knew mighty little about Dorinda Robiseau—not where she came from, who she was, nor where she planned to go. There was no telling about her, and all I had was my first suspicions that she was a witch woman.

Not that I place much stock in witches. All my life I'd heard tell of them, but I had never seen one, nor anything of their doings that I could swear to. . . .

Somewhere along in there, I sort of dropped off, and the next thing I knew it was daylight.

Broad, bright daylight . . .

The sun on my face awakened me, and I sat up fast and looked about.

A moment there, I couldn't place where I was, and then I saw the girl and she was a-settin' up, too.

"We slept over," I said, "and I was a fool to chance it."

About us the mountain walls lifted up steeply, in jagged, broken slopes. Up these a man on foot could climb, with some struggle and skill. Before us, and to the south, the desert lay open, masked only by a drift of sand, a pair of crowded Joshuas, and some small brush. On the horizon to the south, maybe twelve to fourteen miles off, were the Pinto Mountains.

The cove in which we were hidden comprised maybe an acre of flat ground and banked sand. There were some good graze plants in the bottom, and I had the five horses pegged out among them. Sand had heaped across the opening of the cove so that with the brush and all it was mighty near invisible from the outside, without a man riding up to the top of the sand hill.

It was that which saved us, that and the wind being so that none of the horses caught scent of one another. For when I went up to the top of the sand I could see those riders out there, not fifty yards away, and all bunched together, talking.

During the night there had been a wind stirring, not much, but enough to drift sand in this locality where it was loose, and our trail had drifted over. Evidently they had lost track of us and were talking it over to decide which was the most likely route for us.

The side of the mountain was drifted deep with that loose white sand. In some places it looked fit to bury whole sections of the range. So anybody taking a quick look our way would think there was nothing anywhere around but sand and rock.

Me, I motioned back to Dorinda to be still, and I lay there flat out on the sand with only the top of my head showing, and it screened by low brush and the base of a Joshua tree. My Winchester was with me, looking one-eyed at those men down there, ready to speak its piece if they started our way.

There was argument going on among them, but I could only guess at the words. Finally they turned and rode off toward the east and the spring at Twenty-Nine Palms.

That was the next worst thing to their finding us, because there was no nearer water that I knew of, and our canteens were shaking light with only mouthfuls of water remaining.

Lying there in the sand, I watched them ride off.

By the time they reached Twenty-Nine Palms they would figure it out that they were ahead of us, and the chances were they would sit right there by the water and wait for us, knowing that sooner or later we had to show up.

Oh, they would have it figured, all right! They would know about how much water we carried, and about how fast we used it, and right this minute they could guess within a quart the amount of water we had now . . . maybe closer.

So I watched them ride away, and I knew that, riding away in the direction we must go, they carried our lives along with them. It was no easy thing, seeing them ride off, knowing the girl behind me was depending on me for a way out; and when I thought of what tomorrow would bring—the sun, the dust, the miles upon miles of desert around—I felt fear.

But there was no sense in starting off into the blazing heat of a desert day. With them ahead of us, I could, for the first time, choose our time of travel. Taking up my rifle, I slid down the sand, and then walked back to where Dorinda was resting. From my expression she must have realized that trouble was upon us. She sat up, and, dropping to one knee on the sand, I told her.

There are men who prefer to keep trouble from a woman, but it seems to me that is neither reasonable nor wise. I've always respected the thinking of women, and also their ability to face up to trouble when it comes, and it shouldn't be allowed to come on them unexpected. Many a man has sheltered his wife from his troubles, until suddenly he dies and she awakens to poverty as well as grief. So I gave it to Dorinda hard and cold.

I drew her a diagram on the sand. "This here is Twenty-Nine Palms, and beyond is the San Gorgonio

Pass to the coast of the western sea. Right about there is Los Angeles."

"Aren't there other water holes? In some other direction?"

"More'n likely . . . but finding them wouldn't be easy."

She looked up at me. "We'll have to try, won't we?"

Simple as that. Sure, we'd have to try, because as well as I knew anything, I knew those men who had been trailing us would soon know they'd passed us somewhere and, as I'd thought when I watched them ride away, they would just wait for us there by the water.

Making some fire, I burned off the spines from some cholla and beaver-tail cactus and the horses ate them eagerly, for the pulp was moist. In Texas I've known ranchers to feed their stock that way. In this case, I was thinking more of the water they would get from it.

There was shade in the cove, and we sat tight, letting the day move slowly past. I'd made up my mind to travel no more by day, for, without anybody chasing us, there was no reason. Traveling in full desert sunlight can kill a man or a horse mighty quick without enough water . . . and we hadn't enough.

We did no talking, but I did a lot of thinking.

One time in Prescott I'd heard Paul Weaver yarning about some Mojaves who raided the California ranchos for horses and on their way back were driven from the trail by a sandstorm. With them was a Chemehuevi Indian who guided them to a hidden valley and a water hole in the canyon behind it.

This was in a country covered with Joshua trees and a weird lot of rocks piled up in all sorts of strange shapes. Near the valley there had been one

formation I remembered Weaver telling about—
he said it looked like a huge potato balanced on three
points of rock.

There had been two other water holes he mentioned, but of their location I knew nothing—only
that the Chemehuevi had known of them. It was
almighty little to begin with, and I was scared.

Twice I went back up to that ridge of sand and
looked off to the south, and neither time did my
looking give me any room for hope. All I could see
was miles upon miles of empty sand or burning rock,
mostly dotted with creosote bushes, or here and there
cactus or Joshua trees.

When the sun was almost down I put the saddles
on our horses, and loaded up our pack horse. Believe me, those horses were ready to go. They had
sense enough to know that if we were to get out
alive we had to travel. And so, with the dying sun
like a red ball of fire over the western mountains,
we rode over the sand ridge and headed south into
the empty, unknown desert.

After a while a bright star showed up, hanging
above the distant mountains, and I chose it for our
own, putting my horse's nose on it, and pointing it
out to Dorinda.

"What mountains are those?"

"I don't rightly know. Could be the Pinto Range.
There's a dozen small chains of mountains through
here . . . they all look alike the first time you see
them."

"You are risking your life because of me."

"Didn't figure on it."

Beauty does something for a woman—some of
them, anyway. Taking a side glance at Dorinda, I
could see that even out here she'd made an effort
to brush up and comb out. For a girl who'd been
riding and sleeping out, with no water and all, she

looked almighty pert. And I could imagine how I looked, a tall man with a big-boned, wedge-shaped face, a scar on my cheekbone, and by now a heavy growth of beard. Nobody ever claimed I was pretty, but by now I sure must look like an old grizzly coming out of hibernation. The only brushing up I'd done was to beat the dust off my hat and wipe my guns off careful.

Only two things a man really needs in this country to survive, a gun and a horse. . . . Come to think of it, though, there is something else.

Water.

Dorinda was thinking of it, too. She rode up beside me again and said, "However can we find water out there?"

"We've got to be lucky. In desert country you can find it up a canyon, or somewhere where the rock is faulted, or at the lowest point of a basin. But unless a body sees trees out in the bottom, I'd not chance that.

"Sometimes where a ridge pushes into the desert you'll find water, but mostly you look for trees or brush of a kind that needs water. Palm trees grow with their feet in the water and their head in the sun—that's what they say. It usually is only a little way to water if you see palms growing. Willows, cottonwood . . . they are good indicators, too.

"But you can't rely on that. Mostly a body should look for animal tracks, or birds flying, but mostly for bees. I've found that bees can lead a man to water faster than anything, but it's chancy . . . it's chancy."

I felt pretty sure there probably weren't five water holes within a hundred square miles . . . not that you could rely on. Tilting my hat brim down, I studied those hills. It was a cinch we weren't going to find anything this side of the mountains.

The night was cool. The stars hung bright above us, and the horses moved ahead, walking with a steady, distance-eating gait. Several times I opened my mouth and drank in great gulps of that cool air.

An hour passed, and then another. But the mountains seemed no nearer. We were out on the bare desert, and I worried over every bit of talk I'd heard of the Mojave, trying to recall anything that might be of help.

When, judging by the stars, two hours more had gone by, I drew up and got down, and helped Dorinda from the saddle. She was dead beat, I could feel it in her, and she sank onto the sand and just stayed there whilst I swapped saddles and talked encouragement to the horses. They were going to need it.

"How far have we come?" she asked.

"Maybe twelve miles, if you figure a beeline. More, by the way we've had to travel."

"How much further to the mountains? We'll rest then, won't we?"

"We won't rest until we find water . . . if we do."

She got up into the saddle again with some help from me, and we started on, only this time I walked. At least, I walked for the first couple of miles. When I began to stumble, as near asleep as awake, I climbed into the saddle myself.

Sometime after that, I dozed in the saddle, and when my eyes opened again the horses had stopped and it was gray in the east.

We had come up to a deep, sandy wash. Looking around, I saw that witch woman, looking like nothing but a tired girl, just sagging in the saddle and hanging on by sheer grit. My pack horse was gone.

Staring back over the desert, I figured I could see something back there, a black spot of something on the sand.

"You got anything in that outfit of yours that you can't afford to lose?" I asked.

She looked up at me, staring stupidly for a moment before the sense of the words reached her. Then she turned to look, and after a moment she shook her head.

"He may come on after us," I said. "It'll be in him to come after the other horses if he's able. They've been carrying more weight, but they're better stuff than him."

Looking up at her, I added, "Ma'am, you've got some solid stuff in you, too. You surely have."

But her lips were cracked and swollen, and there was no more spark to her than nothing. Nor in me, neither.

Right and left I looked, seeking a way through that wash. The banks were steep, and I feared to slide my horses down for fear they'd never get up after reaching bottom. At last I saw a place that looked like a broken-down bank, so I turned and headed for it. The sky was already lighter, and without water we would last no time in our condition if the sun caught us here.

We got through the wash, although I had to dismount and bully and harry the horses to get them up the opposite bank. A break in the mountains showed ahead of us, and I headed for it. From somewhere there came a burst of energy . . . most likely the last I had.

The sun was an hour old before we found shelter in the lee of a shoulder of rock. That horse of hers just quit cold, and I didn't blame him.

Dumping our saddle gear in the shade of the rocks, I stared around. There wasn't even a barrel cactus within sight, although this was the country in which they grew. Nor was there anything I could use to feed the horses or to give them a bit of moisture. There was nothing but creosote, and mighty little of that.

Sizing up those horses, I could see they weren't going to travel much further, for they were used up. Two of them, the big stallion and my own original horse, might go on for a while. Even the second horse I'd bought from Hardy . . . but that was a question. We had to have water.

Dorinda had slumped over on the sand, but me, I walked out a ways from where she lay and studied the sand. For about an hour I crissed-crossed back and forth over the desert around and about, studying for tracks. Mighty few were to be seen, and none of them were bunched up and traveling the same route, which might indicate water.

Most desert creatures get along either without any water at all, or on mighty little, getting what moisture they need from what they feed on, be it plants or animals. But most will take water when they can get it, and some of them have to have it.

Finally I gave up and came back and sat down. I must have dozed off; when I woke up my throat was so parched I could scarce swallow, and when I tried to open my mouth I could feel my lips cracking with dryness. My tongue was like a stick in my mouth, and I knew our time was short.

The girl was asleep, or maybe passed out. I didn't look to see. One of the horses was stretched out on the ground, the others slumped three-legged, their heads hanging. My face felt stiff, and when I moved my eyeballs they seemed to grate in their sockets.

Catching hold of a rock, I pulled myself up and decided to try it one more time. And like before, I taken up a canteen and slung it around my neck where it couldn't slip off.

We'd slumped down at the foot of a great chunk of white granite, off by itself from the foot of the mountain. Others like it were around, and, starved for water though I was, I had sense enough to fix the shape of it in my mind . . . else I might never find my way back. Not that it was going to matter, if I didn't find water.

"I'll find water," I said out loud.

If she heard me at all, she gave no sign of it, but just lay there on the sand. So I turned and walked off.

The desert sand was white and hot, and the sunlight blazed back from the sand into my face and there was no shielding myself from it. After I had taken only a few steps I began to stagger. Once I fell against a rock and stood there for several mintues, I guess, before I got started again.

My eyes were on the sand, for I was hunting tracks. But something buzzed in my brain—something like an alarm bell of some kind—and then it was gone. Pausing, I felt my eyes blinking and I made my head turn, and there was a man standing on a rock some distance off.

As my eyes focused on him he lifted a rifle, sunlight glinted on the barrel, and he fired. Instinct made me grab for my gun, but the movement overbalanced me and I fell. That much I remember . . . and then nothing else for a long time.

Cold . . . I was cold.

Feebly, I tried to burrow into the sand for warmth, but warmth would not come. My eyes opened, and I tried to swallow. My throat was raw, and the membranes of it chafed and tightened with the attempt.

Somehow I got my hands under me and lifted myself up. It was night, it was cold, and it was very dark. Stars were out, a chill wind was blowing . . . but I was alive.

Alive . . .

I started to crawl.

Suddenly a coyote yapped weirdly, not very far off, somewhere among the rocks, and I stopped.

When I started to crawl again something moved near me and something clicked on stone.

I knew that sound. A hoof . . . but not a horse.

Forcing my stiff neck to bend, I looked up and saw it there, black against the sky for an instant. A bighorn sheep. . . .

In the half-delirium that clouded my brain I felt irritation at the thought of the name. The bighorn was no more a sheep than I was. It was a deer. It had a body like a deer, hair like a deer . . . even the same color. Only the horns were different.

I crawled on, and the blood started moving within me. Pain awakened, I felt raw and torn inside, my body ached.

The bighorn would have to have water, so there must be water near. Forcing my muddled thoughts into line, I struggled to think more clearly. The bighorn had gone into the canyon, so the water must be there . . . at this hour he would be joining others of his kind at water, or would be leaving it.

Somehow I moved on, and then all movement ceased. Something stirred in me and I tried to move on, but I could not.

And then I felt the sun upon my back, and it was hot, terribly hot. My eyes opened and I struggled. In my mind was terror—terror of death, terror of dying here, like this. . . . And there was memory of the sheep. Pulling myself to hands and knees, I stared blearily around for tracks, and found none, for I had crawled upon the rock, bare rock where I saw not even the scars from hoofs.

Suddenly something buzzed by me and sang off into the distance.

A bullet? The sound lasted too long.

Struggling on, I paused again, hearing a queer, cricket-like sound. I knew that sound. It was the croaking made by the red-spotted frog.

And I knew something else. The life of that frog was lived in canyons or in places near permanent springs or seeps.

Water was near.

With a lunge, I came to my feet as though pricked with a knife point. Wildly, I stared around, and saw nothing.

And then that sound again . . . something buzzed by me that I knew for a bee. Quickly I started after it, taking three faltering steps before realizing that the sound had died away.

Scrambling and falling among the rocks, I came upon it suddenly—a basin in the white granite, filled to the brim with water . . . and it was no mirage.

I crawled down to it and splashed water into my face, then scooped a handful into my mouth and held it there, feeling the delicious coolness, and then the actual pain as some trickled slowly down my throat.

It seemed a long time that I lay there, letting that one gulp of water ease down my raw throat. And then after a bit I tried again.

The sun was blistering hot on the granite where I lay, so I crawled into the shade alongside the water. There was room to stretch out there. Several times I drank . . . once my stomach tried to retch.

When perhaps an hour had passed, I began to think.

The girl was back there . . . Dorinda. She and the horses . . .

But there had been a man who shot at me. Or had that been delirium?

Weakly, I struggled to sit up, and then I filled the canteen. I was going back.

I had to go back. I had to know.

four

My old tracks were on the sand to guide me, and I
found the place where I had fallen in attempting to
draw and return the fire of the man with the rifle.
There was a rock where such a man might have
stood, some distance off, but in plain sight. Around
where I had fallen there were no tracks but my own.

More carefully now—for it might not be delirium
that the man had shot at me—I moved among the
rocks of white granite toward the place. . . .

Gone . . .

Dorinda was gone, my horses were gone, my
packs and my gold were gone. Nothing was left.

There had been four or five riders, and they had
approached from the west. They had taken Dorinda,
my Winchester, my horses—and they had vanished.

They must have believed me dead. Here I was,
alone, on foot, and miles from any possible help.

Standing there in the partial shade of that rock,
I knew that I was in more trouble than I had ever
been in my life. I had a canteen of water and a
pistol with a belt of ammunition. But I had no
horse, no food, and no blanket. The nearest settle-

ment of which I knew was maybe a hundred miles away to the west—a Mormon town called San Bernardino.

For the moment my canteen was filled with water, and I had recently drunk. The tank that I had found in the rocks was a half-mile back up the draw; if I retraced my steps and camped there for the night I should have walked a mile to no purpose.

Pa, he always taught us boys to make up our minds, and once made up, to act on what we decided, and not waste time quibbling about. So I taken up my left foot and stepped out toward the west and followed it with my right, and I was on my way.

But I wasn't going far at midday, which it was by now. So I walked on from one of those islands of rock to another, sometimes resting in the shade a mite, then going on to another one, but always holding to the west. And away down inside me I began to get mad.

Until then I hadn't been mad, for we Sacketts, man and boy, are slow to anger, but when we come to it we are a fierce and awful people.

Another thing Pa had taught us boys was that anger is a killing thing: it kills the man who angers, for each rage leaves him less than he had been before—it takes something from him.

When that black-eyed girl back there at Hardyville asked me to help her get on to Los Angeles, I suspicioned trouble, but woman-made trouble, nothing like this. Now those men who chased after her had got her, and they had shot at me, left me for dead. They had taken my outfit and my gold.

Well, now, that was enough to make a body upset. Seemed to me this was a time for anger, and it came upon me. It was no wild, fly-off-the-handle rage, but a cold, deep-burning anger that pointed me at them like a pistol.

They would have gone to Los Angeles, but no matter. Wherever they had gone, I would find them.

A journey, somebody said, begins with one step, so I taken that step. I was started, and before I set my foot down for the last time on that journey there would be blood on the moon.

At sundown I struck out, headed westward. My life depended on getting to water before my canteen emptied. By now they had probably left the Palms, but that was away off to the north and beyond my direction now. I was going to hold westward, and hope.

A man afoot can walk a horse down. It has been done many a time, and while I had no idea of walking them down, if I could come up to water and find food I'd not be far behind them when they reached Los Angeles.

Food . . .

My stomach was already chafing my backbone from hunger, and my belly sure was thinking my throat must be cut, it had been so long since I'd eaten. Nonetheless, I just kept picking my feet up and putting them down.

We mountain boys were all walkers. Mostly it was the fastest way to get ary place back in the hills, for often a boy could cross a mountain afoot where no horse could go . . . if he owned a horse, or even a mule.

Westward the mountains lifted up maybe a thousand feet above the desert, but I'd crossed higher mountains, and if I couldn't go through, I'd go over.

Due west I walked, keeping a steady pace for upwards of an hour, then resting a few minutes and going on again. Two, three times I found rough going that held me up, but by moonrise I was close to the mountains and I picked out a narrow Indian trail or sheep trail. It showed white against the desert and between the rocks; I'd followed many such, and recognized it for what it was.

Most such trails are narrow, maybe four to eight inches wide, and usually easier to see from a distance than close up. I mean, from a cliff or ridge you can pick them out at quite a distance; but on the ground and close up they are hard to find, unless in regular use. But a body gets a knack for seeing them after a bit.

This one went south along the mountains, and I followed it for about a half-mile until it joined up with a westbound trail that cut into the mountains. Following it over and through the hills I found another spring at the foot of a granite spur that stretched out into a high mountain valley. The spring was marked by two patches of white granite, easy to see against the dark rock of the mountain.

In drift sand close by, I bedded down and made some sleep, after a long pull at the water in my canteen. Come daybreak, I drank from the spring, refilled my canteen, and took off to the westward while the sun was still below the horizon.

It came on me then if I was to eat I'd have to look sharp, or maybe lay out near a water hole of a night and try to kill something that came for water. A sheep would be best, but one more day without grub and I'd tackle a desert wolf or most anything that walked or flew—or crawled, for that matter.

It was about then that I came up to the horse tracks.

There must have been fifty in the lot, maybe more, and they were pretty well strung out. These were not wild stuff, but shod horses, most of them, and they were driven. As near as I could tell, they were driven by two men.

Right away I took to the rocks to study it out. The way it seemed to me, this was no country for an honest man to be driving horses. There were no ranches anywhere within miles, and no occasion for anybody to be moving a herd through here that I could grasp hold of. Anybody moving horses would be likely to keep to well-traveled trails and known water holes.

Then I recalled Old Bill Williams, and what Joe Walker had told me about the characters from Arizona who used to steal horses in California and drive them across the desert to sell in Arizona ... or the other way around. Maybe somebody was still doing it.

Horses meant water; and wherever these horses were going, it was a place known to the drovers, who were heading them right across country *toward* something.

That something must mean a hide-out, a camp. And that meant grub. It also could mean a horse for me.

Hunkered down among those big old rocks, I gave study to the problem. If the men driving the horses were thieves, they wouldn't take it kindly of me to come upon them, and they might start blasting at me with firearms. Nevertheless, they would have grub, which I needed, and they would have horses.

For maybe a half-hour I held my place, and gave the time to studying the country around. You never saw such a jumble of boulders, heaped-up rock, and cactus in your life.

And then of a sudden I recalled what I'd been told about a balanced rock near a Hidden Valley, a rock like a huge potato. For there, not more than a few hundred yards off, was just such a rock.

The trouble was, in a jumble of rocks such as that

a man might look for years and not find the entrance to the valley unless he was mighty lucky, or found some tracks. And there was likely a lookout somewhere up among the rocks. No matter—I had to take my look.

Right at that moment I didn't much care. I was hungry, and I was dead tired, and I had been put upon by the men hunting that woman. They had taken my outfit and they had left me for dead, and before this thing was over they would pay through their hides.

So I started to follow those tracks.

"You huntin' something?"

The voice came out of nowhere. I was smart enough to freeze right in my tracks, and when I looked up I saw a man standing there with a Winchester aimed at my belt buckle. He was a rough-looking character wearing a flat-brimmed hat and beat-up chaps.

"You're damned right I am," I said irritably. "I'm hunting three square meals and a horse."

He chuckled at me. "Now you don't tell me you come all this way afoot?"

"No," I said, "I been set afoot. And when I get up in the middle of a horse I'm headed for Los Angeles to find those who left me."

"You a Los Angeles hombre?"

"Arizona," I said. "I started over here to buy horses and goods to take back, and in Hardyville I ran into this woman."

He lowered his rifle. "You don't look like the law," he said, "so come along. We can feed you, anyway."

He walked over to some rocks and he said, "You've got to crawl." He indicated a hole where two rocks sort of leaned together, and I got down and crawled through the hole. When I stood up, I was inside of Hidden Valley.

From where I could see, it looked to be at least a half-mile long, although some of it may have been out of sight. The two walls of rock, mostly heaped-up boulders, were only a few hundred feet apart. Scattered over the bottom of the valley, there must have been sixty or seventy head of good horses.

This gent who showed me in pointed with his Winchester and we walked along the wall of rock where there were some caves and a spring . . . and lots of bees buzzing about.

There was a smidgin of fire going, and three or four gents sprawled around. They sat up when we came into sight.

"What you got there, Willie?" It was a tall man with some teeth missing. "You caught you a pigeon?"

"You think I'm a pigeon," I said, "you just stack your duds and grease your skids and I'll whup you down to a frazzle. . . . After I've been fed."

So they asked me about it, and I laid it on the line for them, having no cause to lie, and they listened. Only thing I didn't tell them was that last shot fired at me. Seemed to me they'd be more sympathetic if they figured I'd been left afoot a-purpose.

Willie put down his rifle and shook out a cup and filled it with coffee. "Start on that. Even if we decide to shoot you, you'll take it better on a full stomach."

"They'd no cause to set you afoot," the tall man said irritably.

Like the Good Book said, I had fallen among thieves, but they were a rough and ready lot, having no bones to pick with me, and no man likes it to be set afoot.

When I'd eaten a mess of beans, some sourdough bread with honey, and about two pounds of good bacon, I pushed back and relaxed with another cup of coffee.

"We'd better give him a horse, Charlie," Willie said. "If he eats like that we can't pack grub enough to feed him."

Charlie rolled a smoke, and when he had lit up he said, "Did you get a good look at any of those men?"

When I had given a description of them—and I'd not found it necessary to tell about the men killed in the gun battle further north—Charlie looked over at Willie and said, "This here friend of yours has bought himself a packet. I figure we should let him have a horse."

Willie and Charlie Button they were, and known men. Somehow they had come upon this Hidden Valley and were using it to hide stolen stock . . . I had my own hunch about that, believing they had learned of it from Peg-Leg Smith, who devoted more time to horse stealing than to losing mines.

"What I can't figure," I said, "is how you get those horses in here in the first place. That's a mighty small hole for a horse."

I didn't get an answer to this.

"You tell me you like to travel by dark," Willie said. "All right, you rest up today. When dark comes we'll give you a horse and point you right. The rest is up to you."

"I'll be obliged."

They never said ary a word about me saying nothing about their hide-out, nor did they need to.

Sure enough, Willie showed me out through the same hole by which I crawled in, and when we got outside there was Charlie and a couple of others with a fine-looking sorrel horse.

"The horse is yours," Charlie said. "You ride him on out of here."

Well, I couldn't avoid it somehow. I just looked at Charlie and said, "How good is my title to this horse?"

Charlie grinned at me. "If you're ridin' west your title is good; if you're ridin' toward Arizona, it ain't good."

Title or not, those boys loaned me a good horse. He just reached out those long legs of his and went away from there, and with the bait of grub they packed for me, I made an easy ride of it.

The hotel of Mr. Gabriel Allen was the place to put up, and when I'd paid my bit from the few dollars of gold in my pockets, I arranged for a bath and bought a razor and soap.

Nobody had got at the money in my pockets, carried for day-to-day expense, so now I went the whole hog and spent twelve dollars for a new suit of clothes. Things seemed almighty high here in the city, for I could have bought the same suit in Prescott for ten dollars. Of course, this wasn't actually the city—Los Angeles was still thirteen or fourteen miles off—but prices were the same. I spent another dollar and a half for a white shirt, and when the man offered to throw in a necktie if I bought two more, I did so.

A boy on the corner blacked my boots for a nickel, so when I finally mounted up to ride into Los Angeles I was dressed for the city, and looked elegant enough for any of those fine homes along San Pedro or Main streets.

So I rode into town and put up at the Pico House, which was the biggest, finest-looking building I ever did see. It had been opened in 1870, and was all of three stories high and built of blue granite. It stood right on the corner of Main Street and the Plaza.

The room they gave me was almost as large as our whole cabin back in the mountains, and when I had brushed up and combed my hair again, I checked my gun. Somebody owed me some horses, thirty pounds of gold, and a couple of good saddles, and I was going to have them back.

Little was my worry over that black-eyed witch girl, for once free of the desert I'd an idea she could care for herself. And so far as she knew, I was dead back there on the sand of the Mojave.

Nonetheless, it was up to me to find out if she was getting a fair shake, and in the way of doing that I would have my gold back, and my horses.

This was the biggest town I ever did see, and I'd suspect there were all of ten thousand people in it. I've heard tell of bigger towns . . . come to think of it, New Orleans was bigger; but that had been long ago, and far away.

It seemed to me no town was large enough to hide that black-eyed woman, and I was right.

First person I saw when I came down stairs into the main lobby of the Pico House was Dorinda Robiseau.

She was across the room from me and she was talking to two men, dressed-up city folks. One of them was a big young man, handsome as all get out, but somehow he looked to me like a shorthorn. Although that slight bulge on the right side of his waist in front gave me to wonder. The other man, maybe fifty-odd years old, was shorter and square-shouldered.

Walking up to them, I said, "Ma'am, I'm glad to see you made it all right."

Her back had been toward me and there was an

instant when it stayed toward me. Then she turned and looked me right in the eye and said, "I beg your pardon? Were you speaking to me?"

The two men who stood with her both looked at me as if I had crawled out from under a log. The big young man started to speak, but I said, "When I got back and found you gone, I was some worried."

"I am afraid," she spoke coolly, "you have made a mistake. I have no idea who or what you are talking about."

Well, I started to explain. "Why, out there in the Mojave, ma'am, I—"

The young man broke in on me. "You heard the lady. She doesn't know you."

He turned his back to me and took her by the arm, and they walked off and left me standing there.

Felt like a country fool, I did, them turning from me like that, and when I glanced around several people were looking at me and smiling with amusement. Made me mad, deep down. And me, traipsing over the desert, fighting and all to get her to safety, and then turned down like some stranger!

The more I thought of it the more it irritated me, and then it came over me that whilst I'd found her, I still hadn't my outfit back. I started to follow after them, but they were gone, clean out of sight.

There was a black carriage going away from the hotel, and mayhap they'd stepped into that.

Anyway, I was going to get my gold.

There were a hundred and ten saloons in Los Angeles about that time, but the one I'd been told to head for was Buffum's. It was the place to hear things, and was the most elegant in town. Buffum's ... that was the place.

Putting on my hat I stepped outside, and as I did so a man moved up beside me. He was a slender, dark young man. A Mexican ... or a Californian.

He spoke to me quietly. "It is of a possibility, señor, that we have interests in common."

"You're doing the talking."

"It is said the dark-eyed señorita has been ill, and confined to her room. I think this is untrue. I believe she left Los Angeles and was brought back."

"Mister," I said, and I stopped and looked at him with no pleasant thoughts in my mind, "I expect what the lady does is her business."

"Ah? Perhaps. The señor is gallant, but is he also wise? The lady is not to be trusted, señor, nor those about her. And they are dangerous. Dangerous to me, but just as dangerous to you also. They will try to kill you."

It went against my nature to hear evil spoken of a woman, yet had I not myself figured her for a witch woman?

"We can talk at Buffum's," I said, "if you've got anything to say. I figure there might be somebody there that I'm hunting."

"There are a hundred and ten saloons in Los Angeles, of which Buffum's is only the finest, not necessarily the best place to look."

Maybe . . . anyway, it was a place I'd heard tell of, and a place to start. Meanwhile, I had pondering to do. And it just might be this gent with me could point out some trail sign I'd missed. Leastways, he knew the town, and I did not.

It came over me that he was probably shaping truth when he declared that black-eyed girl was not to be trusted. But she had been running scared . . . of *what*?

Thinking back, I recalled something Hardy had said that night when I bought the horses from him before crossing the river. When he learned my name was Sackett he advised me not to tell Dorinda. Why was that? What had my name to do with it?

At a table in Buffum's we ordered beer and sat back to watch. The place was crowded with a mixed lot of Spanish men and frontiersmen, businessmen and farmers.

"I was born here," my friend commented suddenly. "My name is Roderigo Enriquez. I love this place, but it is changing, changing too much for my people."

As he spoke I saw across the room a man who looked like one of those I had seen that last night in Hardyville. He stood at the bar in conversation with another man whom I could not see because of those between us.

"My people are not thrifty," my companion went on, "and life in California has been too easy. They have not had to think about money, and there has always been enough to eat; so they are not able to compete in business with the Yankees. The lucky families are those into whom Yankees have married, yet even that is not always enough. As in our own case."

About that time I wasn't paying attention the way politeness demands, for I had my eyes on that man across the room. I was feeling the pistol on my hip, and was ready to move to follow him if he started to leave.

"The Yankee who married into my family was a pirate."

"I've heard of him. Joseph Chapman."

"No, this is another man. Señor Chapman is a good man, and he is a good citizen. My grandfather, Ben Mandrin, is like him in some respects. Only my grandfather was very much a pirate, and a very hard man . . . except to his family."

The man across the room finished his drink and he was not ordering another.

Shifting in my chair, I made ready to rise, but

Roderigo seemed not to notice. "My people lived too easy for too many years, and now that they must compete they lack the capacity. We will lose much."

"Sit tight. Just hang on."

"No, it is not enough. The drouth we have had for two years now . . . it has placed us in debt. And my grandfather signed a note for a friend, the bank failed, and the note will soon be due. We cannot expect an extension."

Me, I was scarcely listening. My attention was all centered on the man I figured to follow, once he started to leave.

"It was Dorinda Robiseau who got him to sign the note."

That stopped me. All Roderigo had been saying had seemed small talk, had seemed like something far away from me, for I had no California land, nor did I know anybody who had any. Now it suddenly seemed to tie in somehow.

"You mean she done it a-purpose?"

"One cannot always prove what one knows, but I believe there was agreement between the directors of the bank and the man with whom Dorinda Robiseau is working. I believe that she got my grandfather to sign the note for his friend when plans had been made to allow the bank to fail."

It made a kind of sense, what he said. The bank was already in a bad way, due to drouth and the resulting loss of cattle and crops. With the bank in serious trouble, if a man showed up offering a chunk of gold money and a chance to get out from under the crash—why, those bankers would be apt to accept . . . if they had larceny in them.

Yes, this made a crooked sort of sense. All the banker had to do was go to his friend Ben Mandrin and get him to sign a note . . . with Dorinda to help.

Those old-time California folks were mighty free-handed with money . . . one man used to keep a big kettle full of it in his patio, and anybody who needed any just dipped in and helped themselves. They were pleasant, easy-going folks and living was no problem. Those around them were much as they were, so it worked out all right . . . until the gold rush and the boom that followed brought another type of man into the country.

The miners and the settlers came first, and most of them were as free-handed, when they had it, as the Californios. After them came the gamblers, the confidence men, the business swindlers.

"How much land is at stake?" I asked Roderigo.

"Over one hundred thousand acres."

It taken my breath away. In the mountains we farmed a hundred and sixty acres, and had as much around that was brush and timber, too steep to farm. Out of that quarter section that we farmed we made a bare living, for there was thin soil and poor crops. But this was rich land, if irrigated.

It was no wonder they were prepared to do murder to win their game, and they could not afford to have me about stirring up trouble.

"That girl, now. What was her part in all this?"

"Old Ben is no different from the rest of us. He likes young, pretty women, and when Turner—he was the banker—came to see him he brought his 'niece' along with him."

The man at the bar turned suddenly and walked from the room, so I got up. "You save the rest of that," I said. "I've got business to attend to."

He had gone off down the street, and when I stepped out and got to the corner I saw him standing in front of what used to be the Bella Union Hotel. They'd changed the name of it to the St. Charles, but it was a place I knew. Ten, fifteen years before there'd been a big gun battle there where Bob Carlisle shot it out with the King brothers.

Anyway, that man was standing there and I started for him, figuring to get just as close as I'd need to be before he saw me. He was a little distance off, but I have long legs and I stepped fast but easy, not to scare him off.

Then he saw me and, turning, he ducked into an alley, and I went in after him . . . too fast.

As I wheeled around the corner, he was standing maybe forty feet off, and he ups with his six-shooter and let drive at me. It was point-blank range, and he should have nailed me, but he'd been running, then just skidded to a stand and fired, so he must have been a mite unsteady.

Something hit me a wallop on the head and I went down to my knees, then fell over, face down on the ground.

From somewhere I heard running feet coming up behind me, and then in the other direction, plain as a body could wish, I heard a door slam.

five

When I hit ground it seemed to me I was only there about a second when folks were all around me filling the breathing air with foolish questions. Lurching to my feet, I fell against the side of the building and leaned there with blood running into my eyes, trying to bring my brain into focus. All I could remember was the sound of a door slamming somewhere down the alley ahead of me.

Folks kept nagging at my attention with questions as to what happened and who shot me, but their words reached me without registering any effect. What little awareness I had was concentrated on just one idea: finding the man who shot me.

Roderigo was there trying to help, but I brushed him away. I got my two feet under me and pointed myself down that alley.

There was only one door in sight. When I got to it I leaned against the wall for an instant, sort of gathering myself for whatever was to come, and then I grasped the latch and opened the door.

The hallway down which I looked was maybe forty feet long, with two doors on the right and one on the left. The first door on the right opened into an empty store building with lumber piled on the floor, as if for building work. There was nobody in the room.

Closing the door as softly as I could, I went on to the next door on my right, which led into a clothing store. The place was empty but for the clerk and one customer.

"Did anybody come through here?" I asked.

They both looked at me, then shook their heads. "Nobody . . . ain't been a soul around," said the clerk.

The door on the left remained, and I turned to it. Opening it suddenly, I stepped inside.

Behind a desk sat the man I had seen with Dorinda Robiseau, the big young man who had guided her away from me.

"You wished to see me?"

"I wish to see the man who came in here from the alley," I said.

"I am very sorry. Nobody has come here. Is that all?"

With my left hand I wiped blood from my face. My skull was throbbing with an enormous and awful ache, hurting so that I squinted when I looked around.

There was just this big rolltop desk, two chairs, and a table. But there was another door.

"Who's in there?" I asked.

"Nobody."

He didn't like me, not even a mite. He started to say more, but I pointed at the door.

"You open it up," I said.

He leaned back in his chair. "Don't be a damned fool. I shall do nothing of the kind. Now you get out of here or I'll have you jailed . . . and I can do it."

Stepping over to his desk, I leaned across it, and I am a tall man. "Mister," I spoke mighty gentle, "you do what you're told."

He got mad then, and he started to get up. Oh, he was a man used to having his own way; it was written all over him. He was a big man and strong, and he was mad. So he started to get up, and when he was off the chair with both his hands on the arms, I caught him by the front of his shirt and vest and jerked him toward me to get him off balance, and then I shoved him back, hard.

He hit that chair and both of them went over on the floor, and I stepped quick to that door and jerked it open. Two bullets came through, their reports one right behind the other, but I was well over to one side and both missed.

That man inside the room, he had just shot into the opening door, taking no aim at all, nor seeing anything to shoot at.

"Next time," I said, "I'm going to shoot back. You going to drop that gun, or are you going to die?"

He didn't seem to like the choice much. I heard him shift his feet, and I said, "You got you two bullets. You might nail me, but I've got five and I'm not about to miss."

"I've nothing of yours," he said, and with my gun up I took a long chance and stepped into the door with my gun in my hand.

He had a notion to shoot, but when he saw that big six in my hand he had another notion that beat that first one all hollow. He taken a long look at that gun and he stepped back and dropped his pistol.

"I ain't about to pick it up," I said, "and you go ahead, if you're of a mind to."

Behind me I heard a stirring on the floor, and I

moved so I could keep half an eye on that big man on the floor, too.

"Mister," I said, "my outfit has been taken. My horses and gold are gone. Now, I aim to have them all back. You boys can start talking or start shooting, and I ain't of a mind to care which."

The big man got up off the floor, but carefully, holding himself with knowledge that I might have a touchy finger on a hair-trigger. With my gun muzzle for a pointer I moved the second man over alongside the first.

"We know nothing about it," the big man said. "I have no idea what you are talking about."

"I think you're a liar," I said, "and if it proves out I'm wrong, I'll apologize and welcome. But this gent who taken some shots at me, he was there. He was in the desert."

"You've got me all wrong!"

"I sure have. And being in the desert, you know I ain't a-fooling when I hold this gun. I want my outfit, and I'm going to have it."

"You're a fool," the big man said contemptuously. "You have that gun on us, but when you leave the law will be on you, and if you shoot us, you'll hang."

"Before I hang," I said, "I'll do some talking."

They didn't like that. They didn't like it even a little. Suddenly I had a feeling that if they hadn't already marked me down for killing, I had just moved myself to the head of the list.

"Watch him, Dayton," the smaller man said, "he's good with that gun."

Dayton smiled, and it was not a nice smile. "My advice to you, my friend, is to get out of town, and get fast."

"Why, I might do that . . . given my outfit."

Dayton glanced at the other man. "What about it, Oliphant? Do you know anything about it?"

Oliphant touched his lips with his tongue. "We figured him for dead. Of course we brought his horses in."

"And thirty pounds of gold," I said.

Oliphant shifted his feet. "I don't know—"

"That's quite a lot, Oliphant," Dayton suggested coolly. "I'd rather like to know about that myself."

"I don't know anything about the gold," Oliphant said. "I—"

Well, I just eared back the hammer on that gun of mine. "You just jog your memory, friend," I said. "You just jog it a mite. If you don't, I'll be asking questions of somebody else."

Oh, he was sweating, all right! He was right-down scared, and not only of me. Apparently he, and maybe some of those others, had just kept still about that gold. But there was still fight in him.

"You'll not talk so loud," he said, "if you brace Sackett."

"Who?"

"Nolan Sackett. And if you don't know that name, you don't know anything. Nolan Sackett, the gunfighter."

He mistook my manner for fear, because I was some startled to hear the name of Sackett. And then suddenly the familiarity of that big-built man returned to me. Not that I knew any Nolan Sackett, nor had I ever heard the name, but the build was so like my own . . . or my brother Orrin's, for that matter, although he was heavier.

There was no Nolan Sackett I'd ever heard tell of, certainly not among the Smoky Mountain or Cumberland Sacketts.

"Clinch Mountain!"

"What's that?" They both stared at me, not guessing what I meant. And knowing no Sackett history, they could not know. But the only kind of Sackett likely to wind up in such a deal was a Clinch Mountain Sackett. They were the outlaw branch, but fighters . . . I'll give them that.

"Mister," I said, "you start talking. Where are my horses and my gold?"

"You'll have to brace Sackett if you want them." He was still thinking the name had scared me. "You ain't about to do that."

"I'll send you to do it," I said, "but if need be, Sackett can face Sackett."

They didn't get it. They just looked at me, so I told them. "Why, Sackett is my name, too. William Tell Sackett, although most call me Tell, and I'm from the mountains of Tennessee, although a different set of mountains from him. And we Sacketts don't take kindly to anyone of our name mixing in with disgraceful conduct. I'll just have to meet this here Nolan Sackett and read him from the Book."

"Your horses are at Greek George's place," Oliphant said, "out beyond Cahuenga Pass. The gold is there, too, if you can get it."

"I'll get it."

Backing to the door, I looked over at Dayton. "You stay out of my way," I said. "I don't like anything about you."

He smiled, but I knew now it was not a nice smile. There was murder in it. "You'll not live to cross the mountains," he said. "I shall see to that."

"You're too busy," I said, "trying to steal an old man's ranch."

That hit him. It was like he'd been slapped across the mouth, and he came up out of his chair, white around the lips, but I just stepped outside and pulled the door to behind me.

Roderigo was waiting for me at the end of the street, and he was worried.

"I was afraid for you," he said. "I did not know what to do."

"First things first. Do you know Greek George's place?"

"Who does not? It is there they captured the outlaw, Tiburcio Vasquez."

"Is it far?"

"Ten miles . . . only that. At the foot of the mountains."

"My horses are there. My gold also."

He glanced at me. "And you will go for them? Do you know what you do, señor? It is the place of the outlaws. And there are outlaws in the canyons all along the Santa Monica Range. You must have the sheriff, señor, and a posse."

"I carry my own posse." I slapped my holster. "And as for a sheriff—why, we Sacketts always figured to skin our own skunks, and ask no help of any man."

"I would ride with you, señor."

Well, I looked at him and figured to myself that this one was pretty much of a man. "You do that if you feel the urge for it," I said; "only come prepared for shooting, if need be."

We went for our horses, and I had an idea we'd be late if we did not hurry, for Oliphant would be sending someone, or riding himself, to warn them.

"There's a man out there name of Nolan Sackett," I said. "If anybody shoots him, it will be me."

His face paled a mite. "I did not know he was there, *amigo*," he said. "It is said that he has killed twenty-two men."

"To have killed men is not a thing of which one can be proud," I said. "A man uses a gun when necessary, and not too often, or carelessly."

We mounted up and rode up Fort Street and out of town, heading west and north along the foot of the mountains, with the land sloping off west and south away from us. We rode past irrigation ditches and orchards, and it gave me excitement to see oranges growing, for I'd never seen more than a half-dozen of them in my lifetime.

The railroad had come to Los Angeles with its steam cars, and looking back I could see a train standing at the depot. Main Street led from the depot through part of Sonora town where some of the poorer Mexican and Californios lived, mostly in white-washed adobe houses. The Plaza was set with cypresses; this side of it was the Pico House and the Baker Block, two of the show places of the town. Most of the streets where folks lived were lined with pepper trees, but when we got away from the irrigation ditches it was almighty dry. Because of the bad drouth the last two years, things were in poor shape. The grass was sparse, and there was little else but prickly pear.

With Roderigo leading, we cut over to the *brea* pits road through La Nopalera—the Cactus Patch*—to a small tavern kept by a Mexican. Roderigo swung down and went inside, whilst I sat my horse outside and looked the country over.

Only the faintest breeze was stirring, and the air was warm and pleasant . . . it was a lazy, easy-going sort of day when a man felt called upon to laze around and do not much of anything. Only we had something to do.

West of us lay the Rancho Rodeo de las Aguas,† but looking along the edge of the mountains I saw a faint smudge of blue smoke, indicating where our destination lay. This was the adobe house of Greek George . . . the very same place where Tiburcio

*The area now known as Hollywood.
†Now the Beverly Hills area.

Vasquez had been shot and wounded as he scrambled out a window, attempting to escape.

Roderigo came out of the tavern, looking serious as all get out. "Señor, there are five men at the house of the *Griego,* but the man of your name is not among them."

Well, I was some relieved. No Sackett had ever shot another, and I wasn't itching to be the first. We'd never had much truck with those Clinch Mountain Sacketts, for they were a rough lot, having to do with moonshining and perambulating up and down the Wilderness Trail or the Natchez Trace for no good purpose. But they were fighters . . . they were good fighters.

"We'll ride over there," I said. "I figure to lay hands on my outfit."

He looked at me, and I'll give him this. He was game. He mounted up and swung his horse alongside of mine, and the only thing he did was to reach back and take the thong off his six-shooter.

"I would like you to meet my grandfather," he said suddenly. "Old Ben would like you."

"From all I've heard," I replied honestly, "I'd like to meet him."

And I'd heard a-plenty. This here was a wise old man, although not too wise to be taken in by a pretty face. But he was not alone in that.

We trotted our horses along the road that came down behind the adobe, and we swung down.

The door opened and a man lounged there, a tough, kind of taunting smile on his face. "Well, look who's here! We figured you were lyin' dead out on the Mojave."

"I take a lot of killing."

"So you do." The man chuckled. "But we never make the same mistake twice."

While he was making talk, I was walking toward

him. Roderigo, so far as I knew, had not moved from his place by the horses.

The man in the door straightened up and, grinning at me, suddenly went for his gun. He no doubt fancied himself a fast man, but I didn't even move to draw. I just fetched him a clout with one of my fists, which are big and toughened by a good many years of work with shovel, sledge hammer, and rope . . . and he never got his gun clear.

My fist caught him on the angle of his jaw and drove the side of his head against the door jamb. He slumped over and fell where he was, and at the same time I heard two quick shots from outside. Flattening against the door with my fist full of gun, I glanced over to see Roderigo holding a smoking pistol. There was a man with a Winchester slumped over a sill of the window in the ell of the house. He looked kind of dead to me.

Inside three men were suddenly reaching for the smoky beams, and a pretty Mexican girl was standing staring at me. She was young, but she was pert . . . and I'd say that her path had probably been a twisty one.

"You look like him!" She was surprised, a body could see that. "You look just like him!"

"We Sacketts favor," I said, "if it is Nolan you speak of, but I've never seen the man."

"You'll see him but once," she said contemptously.

"Why, now. As to that, I'll speak my piece and he'll go about his business . . . elsewhere."

It was not so much a boast as a wish. I called for no shooting with kinfolk, and was surprised that he had it in mind. Only maybe he didn't.

To those others I said, "I came for my outfit . . . and the gold."

"You'll find your horses and gear yonder." A red-

74

headed man indicated the corral and stable. "I don't know anything about any gold."

"Ma'am," I said to that Spanish girl, "stir up your fire. I reckon we're going to need it. And bring that spit over here." I grinned at those men. "I traipsed about down New Mexico way for quite a time. Those there Apaches, they know a thing or two."

The red-headed one, he wasn't worried much, but those others, they started shifting their feet and both of them broke out in a sweat.

The one I'd slugged in the doorway was fetching around, so I backed up and grabbed hold of the back of his neck with one hand and dragged him bodily into the room and skidded him across the floor.

The Mexican girl hadn't moved. I took up a poker and worried the fire a mite, then she turned and took up her shawl. "Don't you worry," she said to the others. "I'll go for Nolan and Señor Dayton."

She looked boldly at me. "This one will do nothing! He is afraid."

I chuckled at that, and it made her mad. Her black eyes flashed and she started to say something back, but I just said, "Ma'am, you sure are a pretty little baggage, but you just go get Nolan Sackett, and when you come upon him you tell him it is William Tell Sackett who is here, and to come along if he's a mind to. As for Dayton, he knew I was coming here. I saw him earlier today . . . with a man named Oliphant."

That surprised them, but she went scooting out like she was afraid I'd stop her, which I'd no mind to do. It was in me to settle things, and if they all came around so much the better.

"I have friends, señor," Roderigo said to me; "perhaps I should go for them." He paused. "There are the vaqueros from our ranch, and I believe it is a thing they would like, to find these . . . who are known to be thieves."

Now even Red was looking out of sorts, so I told Roderigo, "You go ahead. Tell 'em to bring extra rope. We may need some neckties for these boys."

Back in those days the pueblo, as everybody called Los Angeles, was a place noted for being mighty free with their hangings, legal or otherwise. Over a span of a few years there had been forty legal hangings and thirty-seven spur-of-the-moment affairs. Shootings were a daily occurrence, but, casual as the authorities were, the townspeople were notoriously short-tempered on occasion, and it required little effort to organize a lynching party.

They might not figure me for much, but they had the consciousness of their own guilt to worry them.

There was a close-up storeroom at the back of the house and, herding them all back there, I put them in and barred the door.

Outside, I located my horses, all five of them, and my saddle gear. Saddling up the horses, I found my pack, which had been gone through, but most of it nobody wanted and so it was intact. My Winchester I found in the house along with somebody else's outfit. The Winchester I took, checked the loads, and made ready for whatever might happen.

But what I wanted most was the gold, not all of it being mine. And believe me, I wanted what belonged to me. For the better part of an hour I went over that house, going through everything, hunting the gold, but I didn't find it at all.

And then I heard horses a-coming and knew I was in for shooting trouble.

From the window I watched them approach, then slipped outside and waited among the willows beside the spring. The Mexican girl was with them, and I counted six men, all heavily armed.

They came up at a fast trot, accompanied by a little dust cloud, and as they slowed their pace and spread out to surround the house the dust sort of thinned and settled down. When they actually moved up around the house the horses were walking.

Crouched among the willows, I just waited and let them come. I wasn't seeking any shooting war unless forced to it. Most particularly, I was hunting Nolan Sackett, but he wasn't among them.

All this time I was studying about where my gold might be. Oliphant had said it was here, on this place, but I had my doubts.

When those riders dismounted and went into the house I went over to my horses, mounted up on the stallion, and walked them away from there. From inside I heard argument and talk, but I walked steadily away from there, putting the bulk of the barn behind me as soon as I could, and heading for the mouth of a canyon that opened not far off.

Roderigo would be back, and until then I wasn't going to do any shooting I could avoid. I might kill the wrong man. I might kill the man who knew where my gold was.

After a minute or two they came bursting out of the door and began to hunt all around.

Sitting my saddle in a clump of tall cactus, I watched them, holding my Winchester across the saddle in front of me. Off down the valley from the direction of the Rancho Rodeo de las Aguas I could see a dust cloud that meant riders moving fast.

The men at the house started scouting around for my tracks, but there were too many horses around the place, and too many people had come and gone. They weren't going to get anywhere with that, and I wasn't much worried.

I was only worried about getting my gold back, for there were folks back in Arizona depending on me. My hunch was that wherever that gold went, Dorinda would know. Unless I was judging her all wrong, she was a girl who could keep her eye on a thing like that.

That distant cloud was coming nearer, and I guess they sighted it, too, for all of a sudden they scrambled for their saddles and rode off, scattering out.

Two of them rode past me, heading up the canyon* where there were other hangouts for outlaws.

When they had gone I walked my horses from the clump of cactus and rode back down to the ranch. Only the girl remained to greet me, and her eyes flared when she saw me.

"You know where that gold is?" I asked mildly. "You could save me trouble if you told me."

"I care nothing for your trouble!" She tossed her head. "When Señor Sackett comes he will make a fool of you."

"He'd better hurry. My friends are coming."

She said nothing to that, for now we could hear the drum of the horses' hoofs.

"If you change your mind," I said, "you come to me. Seems a shame, a pretty girl like you, mixed up with this crowd."

She started to reply, then tightened her lips.

There were twenty wiry, tough-looking vaqueros with Roderigo, and they looked disappointed when it proved there would be no fight.

"You had better come away with us," Roderigo said, "Old Ben wishes to see you."

"Ben Mandrin?"

"Sí." He smiled. "And the Señorita Robiseau."

---

*Laurel Canyon.

six

The house was a long adobe with several doors opening on a veranda. The place was old and mellow. There were some huge old oaks about, and a few sycamores. The shade was a welcome thing after the long ride's heat, and I pulled up there and sat my saddle a minute or two, just looking around.

If they didn't take it away from Old Ben, this place might become Roderigo's, and I didn't blame him for wanting it. There was a feeling of lazy good will about it, from the smell of the barnyard and the jasmine around the house to the shade of the huge old trees.

The house was L-shaped and rambling, and opened on a view that showed the sea away off to the west—just a hint of it beyond the round shoulder of a hill. In between was grassland, brown now and parched from the drouth, with here and there a cultivated patch of corn or beans, or some other row crop.

A door opened and, looking past my horse's head, I saw Dorinda standing there, wearing a lovely dress and looking more beautiful than she'd a right to.

"Won't you get down and come in? Mr. Mandrin would like to see you."

She turned. "Juan, will you take care of the gentleman's horse?"

Stepping down from the saddle, I whipped dust from my clothes with my hat and walked across the yard. The feeling up my spine warned me that somebody was watching—not Dorinda, and not Juan.

She held out her hand to me, smiling with her lips. It was a wide, pretty smile showing beautiful teeth, but her eyes did not smile. They were cautious, somewhat worried eyes.

"Thank you, Mr. Sackett. Thank you very much for all you did. When they came to get me we thought you were dead."

"Handy," I said.

"What do you mean?"

"Otherwise they might have made sure."

She let her eyes rest on my face a moment longer, as if trying to judge how smart I was, or how dangerous. . . .

"It was all a mistake."

"There's men dead out there on the Mojave would be surprised to hear it," I said bluntly.

When she started to answer me I cut her short. "Ma'am, I didn't come to call on you. I came to see Ben Mandrin."

His voice came deep and booming. "And so you shall! Come in, Mr. Sackett! Please come in!"

He was sitting in a great old rocker, and whatever I had expected a pirate to look like, it was not this. He had never been tall—not like me, anyway—but he was broad-shouldered, and my guess was that he had once been a mighty powerful man. It showed in the size of his bones. His wrists were as large as mine, which are ten inches around, and he had strong, well-made hands, flat across the knuckles . . . a fighter's hands.

He had a broad, heavily boned face and deep-set eyes; his heavy shock of black hair was mixed with gray. He had to be upwards of seventy years old, but he didn't look it. Only you could see at a glance that something was wrong with his legs. He had them covered by a blanket, but I could tell they were thin, almost like there was nothing there at all.

There was an old scar over one eye and another on his cheekbone, but he did not look sinister, as they say of such men. He looked like a strong old man who had lived a life.

He was old, all right, a body could see that, but I could see a whole sight more. Old as he was, and with those crippled legs, there was a lot of iron in him yet.

"So you're Sackett?" he said. "Dorry told me of you. You sound like a fighting man."

The scar over his eye held my attention, and he noticed it. "Saber," he said. "That was a long time ago, a lifetime away."

"Off Hatteras," I said, "and they thought it killed you."

Well, both of them were surprised. Dorinda turned sharply to look at me, and the old man caught the arms of his chair and pulled himself out of his slump. "Now how could you know *that*?" he said. "There were few enough who knew."

"You raided the Carolina coast too often," I said. "The man who gave you that cut over the eye was my grandfather."

He glared at me for a minute, then he chuckled. "He was a fighter," he said. "Best hand with a blade I ever saw—bar one."

81

He took a good look at me. "There's another Sackett here. Is he kin of yours?"

"I reckon. He's a Clinch Mountain Sackett, and we don't hold with them . . . but we aren't pirates."

There was a mighty hard look in those eyes of his . . . gave a man something to think about. Had he been a younger or even a healthier man, you'd think twice before giving sass to him. But I thought he liked this talk, and it came over me that it had probably been a time since anybody gave him back man-talk. Because of his wealth and his being crippled and all, they'd more than likely soft-talk him.

"That was a long time ago," Ben Mandrin said. "I've become a rancher and a stable citizen." His eyes glinted with a kind of tough humor. "Or hadn't you heard?"

"I heard, and I believe it . . . up to a point."

He chuckled again and, glancing over at Dorinda, he said, "I like this man."

Then he turned his eyes back to me. "How'd you like to work for me?"

"I'm not hunting work. I'm hunting thirty pounds of gold that was taken from me, and when I find it I'm riding back to Arizona. And furthermore"—I looked right at Dorinda—"I've got an idea who to ask about it."

Oh, he got it all right! Old Ben missed mighty little. He glanced at her, then back at me. "You're wrong, my friend—she has been with me."

He gestured toward a chair. "Sit down, and we'll talk a bit of ships and sabers and the Carolina coast fifty years ago . . . or how much did your grandfather tell you?"

He turned to her. "Dorinda, bring us a bottle of wine—a very good bottle, that will bring memories around us."

We sat silent then, listening to her retreating footsteps. From the sound of them, the wine must have been somewhere at the far end of the house, and it was a great way off, it seemed.

"You helped her in the desert, Sackett, and for that I thank you."

Surprised, I was, for I'd been thinking he knew nothing of her leaving the pueblo. "I went for water, and when I started back, they had her. I stumbled as one of them shot at me, and he thought me dead."

"And you lay still? She does not know that I know." He lighted a long black cheroot, then gave me a sharp glance. "Did she get your gold?"

"As to that, I couldn't say, but I would believe her a woman to know where gold was. I think"—I tried to put it so he would take no offense—"she has a nose for gold, if you'll not mind my saying so."

She came back then, walking along the veranda toward us, and we sat silent, waiting. The bottle she brought was Madeira, of a kind they call Rainwater, although no storm that I have seen brought such water from the sky.

"I would have preferred Jamaica," he said, "but it is hard to come by in California."

We tasted the wine, and it was good. I thought him a fine old man, but I trusted the wine more than I did Old Ben Mandrin; and I trusted him a bit more than I did that black-eyed witch woman. Surely, I thought, this was a strange way for a tall and homely cowhand and miner to be treated, and it gave me an uncomfortable feeling to think that it was likely he would lose all this.

Roderigo had told me a little more during our ride from the pueblo to Greek George's ranch. Turner, the man from the bank, had relied on Dorinda to persuade Old Ben to sign the notes; and Turner would get cash from Dayton and his friends, while they would take over the note and get the ranch. Even without the note, they would have Old Ben lashed to the mast, for he was broke and down to his last bit of money.

The drought had ruined the crops and his range, and there was nothing left for him but to yield up the rancho . . . but what would he do then, a crippled old man?

There was none of that in his talk now, for once the wine warmed his blood he talked of the old days off the Carolina coast, and of the fight with my grandfather. They had fought on a bloody deck —my grandfather being one of a make-up crew that had gone off to intercept him when there was no warship about equipped to handle the job. They had fought a desperate fight, with both men wounded and bleeding before the cut that felled Old Ben.

As we talked he kept his eyes on me, or looked off and seemed to be listening to the sound of my voice, although it was rare indeed that I had chance to speak. But it seemed to me there was something on his mind, something dark and secret that he held within himself.

Dorinda listened, and occasionally she went from the room and returned. I noticed she drank no wine . . . was there purpose in that? Or did she simply not drink at all? Sometimes she seemed impatient, wishing me to be off, no doubt, for all of our talk was taking us no place.

It was in my own mind to leave, until suddenly Old Ben said, "You must stay the night, Sackett. You can snug down here—there's room enough and more. It will be time enough to go off hunting your gold in the morning."

He looked at me sharply as he replaced his glass on the table. "Roderigo said you had planned to buy mules or horses and pack goods back to the mines to sell. Is that still in your mind?"

"When I have my gold."

He waved his hand at the broad acres around me. "They plan to take all this from me, but there's mules enough, and I could let you have some . . . for a small price. I'll have some run up for you to look upon."

He caught hold of his cane suddenly as if to get up, then stopped and said to Dorinda, "Tell them to come for me, and show Mr. Sackett to a room." He paused again as if thinking. "To Pio's room," he added.

She looked surprised, but left the room, and when she came back two vaqueros came with her. They picked Old Ben up, chair and all, and carried him from the room. When they had gone I finished my wine and put down the glass.

"I have never seen him like this," Dorinda said, puzzled and disturbed. "He has never talked so much to any stranger."

"It was because of the old times," I said. "My mention of the fight off Hatteras brought it all back to him."

Some of her puzzlement seemed to go away. "Yes, yes, that must be it," she said.

She was a beautiful woman, but now I could see a coldness there that I had not noticed so much before, although I was ever wary of her.

"But in Pio's room!" she went on. "He has never allowed anyone in that room but the old governor."

"Pio Pico?"

"They were friends . . . are still friends, I think, although he comes out but rarely now." And she said no more.

There were four of us at supper, Old Ben, Roderigo, Dorinda, and myself, but now Old Ben talked little. He broke in once to say, "There was some shooting around Mora, in New Mexico, in which some Sacketts were involved. One of them married a Mexican girl."

"They are my brothers," I said.

He ate with good appetite, I noticed, but drank no more wine—only several cups of the blackest coffee this side of Hell itself. I drank my own share, but I was used to cow-camp coffee which will float a horseshoe.

Tired, I was, and ready for the bed, and we sat about very little after supper was over.

In my room was a huge old four-poster bed, the finest bed I had ever seen, and on a marble-topped table were a bowl and a pitcher of water. There was a chair and a thick carpet on the stone-flagged floor. The room had one window, and an inner door that evidently connected with Old Ben's room.

Sitting down on the edge of the bed, I considered the situation, and none of it made sense. All I wanted was to get my gold back and get out on the trail back to the mines, yet here I was, a guest in an old Spanish hacienda, the guest of a former pirate.

True, I had my outfit back, but the country was filled with my enemies—and all through no fault of mine. Only trying to help a girl who, it now seemed, was tied in with my enemies . . . enemies I'd made because of her.

Tired of trying to figure it out, and deciding I was pretty much of a fool, I pulled off my boots, washed my face and hands, and started to undress.

And then the door from Old Ben Mandrin's room opened and he stood there, hanging on a pair of crutches, and looking at me with devil's laughter in his eyes.

He swung himself around and lowered himself into the chair. "I need help, boy. I need your help."

Me, I just stood looking at him. He was dressed for riding, in an outfit that had once fitted him, but did so no longer.

"We've got to ride nearly twenty miles before daybreak," he said. "Pull your boots on."

It looked like I was never going to sleep in a bed.

"You in shape for a twenty-mile ride?" I said.

"No . . . but I'll ride it. Leave that to me."

I could only stare at him. "Why me?" I said. "You've got men around. You've got Roderigo." And then I grinned at him. "And you've got Dorinda."

He brushed the suggestion away. "An old man's fancy. Look, son, you're young. You're strong. There will be many women for you, but for me she may be the last. I'll not be saying she's mine, for she isn't, and I am sure she has nothing of the kind in mind.

"She looks like a passionate woman, but she isn't, son. Take it from me, the great courtesans of the past—and Dorinda is like them—were never passionate, loving women. They were cold, calculating. They used the emotions of men for their own purposes, they were all show, all promises. A passionate woman gets too involved for straight thinking, she becomes too emotional . . . not Dorinda. She's thinking all the time."

"Then why not be rid of her?"

"Like I say, she may be the last beautiful woman to pay me attention. Most of us pay for love in one way or another, and I paid for her attentions by signing that note." A wolfish gleam came into those hard old eyes. "Now with your help, I'm going to serve them what they have coming."

"It don't sound right to me."

"That's why I chose you. You're honest."

I just kept looking at him. I'd grown up on stories of him, and I could see they were true. He was an old

devil, but I found myself liking him. And sympathiz-
ing with him, too.

"What you got in mind?" I asked cautiously.

"A ride to the west . . . to a place out in the mountains."

"You're in no shape. Tell me what you want done,
and I'll do it."

The wolf in him showed his teeth. His eyes
danced wickedly. "This I shall do myself." The
smile disappeared. "All I am going to do is save my
ranch, and injure no man."

A moment I thought about it, but I was getting
nowhere. I was no hand to ferret out the plans of
other folks. Maybe I just ain't smart, maybe there
ain't enough wolf in me . . . I don't know. I can face
up to guns or fists, but believe me, I can't plot and
figure out ways to deceive.

No use my trying to study out what he had in
mind. I knew I was going to help him, because if an
old man in his kind of shape had the guts to try to
ride twenty miles, I was going to help him. And I
knew I wanted to see the old devil outsmart those
who would rob him of what was his.

"All right," I said.

"Get horses," he said, "and hurry. We've far to
go."

When I started for the door, he hooked my arm
with a crutch. "The window," he said. "Our doors
will be watched."

The window went up soundlessly, and I eased out
into the still night. Stars were out, and somewhere
an owl talked in a treetop. Moving on cat feet, I
made the corral where my horses were. It taken only
minutes to get them out and saddled, the two best
of them. Then I led them back in the darkness close
to the house.

I managed to get Old Ben through the window, but

he helped me some. When I lifted him to the saddle, I was sure surprised. He was light, but there was power in his arms and shoulders and hands . . . I could feel that.

Mounting up, I led off into the night, and then he took over. He could ride, all right. He put his horse westward into the mountains, and I trailed behind, fearful all the time that he might fall off and hurt himself.

The wind was cool on our faces. The black of the mountains loomed above us. We rode steadily westward, and there was no talk between us, although, worried as I was about him, my eyes kept straying his way. But he rode steadily, although with his weakened, crippled legs, I could not guess how he managed it.

These were dark and silent hills. There were cattle here, and horses, but they slept their own sleep and we saw none of them. Once, we saw distant lights . . . we slowed our pace and walked our horses carefully through the dust so as not to awaken the sleepers in the village surrounding a ranch. In those years much of the population clustered in such tiny villages gathered about the ranches.

We turned suddenly into the mountains, mounting by a narrow trail only faintly seen. The ground was lighter in shade where it was worn by the passing of men or cattle. As we climbed I fancied I could smell the sea; and suddenly, when we topped out upon a ridge, I knew it for truth. There it lay, broad upon our right, the great ocean of the Pacific.

He drew up then and looked seaward. I could not see his eyes in the darkness, but it seemed to me there was a longing in him, a longing for the deep waters.

It was in me to understand this, for I knew my own bit of longing for the wild places. I am a man not

given to cities, nor the crowded walks of men. I
like the long winds upon my face, the stirring of
miles of grass bending before the wind, the cloud
shadows upon the plain, the lure and lift of far hills.

Below us and a little behind us, dark against the
moonlit sea, a point thrust into the waters. He swept
a hand toward it, and along the shore. "Malibu," he
said, "Rancho Malibu."

He glanced at the stars, and pushed on, although
the trail was rough. By the feel of it, it was one
rarely traveled. We dipped into hollows and emerged
from them, and now he seemed to be doing his best
to lose me, to prevent me from ever retracing my
steps.

Suddenly he turned at right angles and dipped
into a gap or pass in the mountains, and when he
had gone but a short distance, he drew up.

"Help me down," he said, as I dismounted.

Reaching up, I lifted him from the saddle, and he
sagged in my arms, then drew back.

"No crutches," he said. "They'd be no use to me
here." Iron came into his voice. "Wait for me here
. . . I shall be a while."

He could not walk, but crawled away into the
black darkness where no moonlight fell. I lighted a
cigar, cupping my hands well to conceal the point
of flame, and prepared to wait.

To what strange place had he brought me? And
why had he crawled off in the darkness alone?

Once, a long while after he had left me, I heard
a stone rattle distantly in the night, and I knew
that it fell off into space, for a long time later I heard
it strike.

I was thinking that old Ben Mandrin was no fool,
and I knew that whatever he did, it was something
he wished desperately to do. But he was no man to
be either questioned or doubted, so I just stayed

there and listened into the night . . . listening both for him, and for trouble that might come.

Several times I glanced at the stars to check the time that passed, and they gave me no comfort. It was a far ride back to the ranch for a tired old man, and daylight might find us on the trail. What then? What if they carried his breakfast to his room and found him not there? Or what if his heart failed on this ride and he died with me? Would anyone believe my story?

Restlessly, I tramped up and down, impatient for his return. Was he only a few yards off, listening, perhaps with amusement, to my restless pacing? Or had he gone far away and fallen, injuring himself? But I heard no call for help, and the night was clear and cool.

Finally, I sat down, lighted a fresh cigar with caution, and waited. I thought of what odd turns there are in the life of a man. It was strange that I should be here with this old pirate of whom I had only heard as a boy, and had known now only a matter of hours.

There were no trees here, only the black chaparral. Some of the bushes were almost as tall as a man, but most no more than waist high, yet there were game tunnels beneath them, trails long used by lion or coyote or bobcat. They formed a maze that covered all this chaparral country with hidden trails, to be followed by wild creatures or by a man, if he chose to crawl. Here, atop this ridge, the chaparral was thin, for the ridge was broken by jagged rock outcroppings or by gigantic boulders, bare and time-eroded.

The stars waned. Impatiently, I ground out the stub of my cigar and got to my feet.

The horses, heads up, ears pointed, were looking off into the night, toward the direction in which Ben

Mandrin had crawled. Nostrils dilated, they looked along the ridge.

Stepping out away from them, I spoke softly, "Ben?"

No answer came.

It was too dark to see tracks, and although I had risked lighting the cigars, to hold a light while trying to make out tracks seemed too chancy. This was a high ridge, and the country was alive with outlaws. If I started out to search for him, I might miss him in the darkness. I had no idea how far he had gone, nor even if he had persisted in the direction in which he started, for that might have been only to give me a false idea.

My head was aching, for the riding had set that wound on my skull to throbbing. It hadn't amounted to much . . . a bullet that cut a furrow in my scalp and skinned away some hair, but it also left a lump there big as a hen's egg.

Waiting had given me time to think, and precious little time I'd had before for pondering. But I still didn't know who had been chasing Dorinda when I first met up with her, or why, although it began to look like she might have wanted to get out of this deal with Old Ben. But why?

What was her stake in all this? And who had got her into it? There must have been something promised to her. . . . And where was Nolan Sackett?

Most of all, where was my gold?

Again I looked at the stars. The hour was late, and there was but little time left to us. I got to my feet and walked off into the darkness, listening.

There was no sound.

He was out there alone, and something had gone wrong, I was sure of it now. It wasn't in me to abide longer with that crippled-up old man out there on the rocks and in the dark of night.

So I started out after him.

We were high up on a hog-backed ridge, with the mountains falling away toward the sea on one side and on the other a deep hollow,* what in this country they call a *potrero*, because usually those hollows are good pastureland. There wasn't much chance of getting lost up here because a man had mighty little room to move around in.

It was the dark hour that comes before daylight, and I worked my way along carefully, straining my eyes to see if he lay on the ground, passed out. A couple of times I called softly, but nobody gave back reply.

Suddenly I came to where the trail, if you could call it so, broke in two, with one way going on along the hogback, the other seeming to go out along the shoulder of an even higher ridge. That last looked a mighty bad place to go.

Here I must take a chance, for there was no time to search out both ways. The ridge would shield any light that showed from the land side, and as for the sea, I'd have to chance it. So, kneeling down, I struck a match, held it cupped in my hands, and checked the ground.

It was there, plain as a skunk on a log. The old man had dragged himself along here and taken that higher ridge trail.

Only it wasn't a trail. It was a thread of rock hung in space over several hundred feet of steep fall. Dark as it was, I couldn't see how far it was, but it was a-plenty. So I started out along that shoulder. After a while the trail widened out, then narrowed down.

I'd walked a couple of hundred yards from my horse before I stopped to call out again. And this

*Where Lake Sherwood now lies, and the valley beyond.

time I heard a faint stirring up ahead of me. Whether it was game animal or man, I couldn't tell, but I moved on, and suddenly there he lay in the trail ahead of me, face down on the rock and sparse grass where he'd been crawling.

His hands were skinned and chewed up from the rocks. Beside him in the trail was a big sack full of something. I wished for the moon, which had gone from the sky a long while back. Well, there was mighty little time, so I scooped him up in my arms, and then reached down and got a hold of that sack, which was fearful heavy. Somehow, sweating and panting, I got them both back to our horses, and loaded up.

He came out of his faint when I was hoisting him up. "Can you hang on, or should I lash you up?"

"You start, boy, and you ride like hell. I'll stay with you."

He grabbed my wrist, and believe me, that old devil still had the power to hurt in that grip of his. "Boy," he said, "I've got to be stretched out in bed before there's anybody afoot at the ranch. Don't you worry about me. You just get me there."

I taken him at his word. Those horses were fixed up and a-raring to go, and we lit out of there fast, high-tailing it down off that mountain.

We hit that little village at a dead run, and a moment after we raced through, somebody ran into the trail and yelled after us, but we headed across the plains toward the ranch. And he stayed with me. Old and weak he might seem, but there was grit in him, and we almost ran the legs off those horses until we were within a hundred yards or so of the ranch.

There was gray in the sky and a light was going in one of the vaquero shacks, but we slipped in, and I got him back through my window. Then I got him into his own bedroom, and he locked the heavy bag in a closet at the head of his bed.

Outside, I hurriedly stripped the gear from the horses and turned them into the corral. Nobody was around, so I rubbed them down, and was working over them when a vaquero came out.

Well, he pulled up short when he saw me there working, but I just raised up and said, *"Buenos dias, amigo."* Then I added in English, "When do we eat around here?"

"Poco tiempo," he grunted, and went inside. So I kept on working over my horses, rubbing them down carefully, then forking hay into the corral, and going to the bin for a healthy bait of corn for each. They'd earned it.

When I walked to the house and stepped up on the veranda, Dorinda was standing there. She gave me a sharp glance and said, "You're up early."

"Now, ma'am," I said gently, "no such thing. You take any mountain boy . . . he'd be apt to be up this early. Why, back to home we'd had the cows milked by this time, or if 'twas winter, we'd be out runnin' a trap line."

"I had no idea you were from the mountains," she said, and I don't know why, but suddenly I knew she lied.

"Have you seen Mr. Mandrin?" she asked.

"Me? Is he up and about?"

She came up close to me. "Tell," she put a hand on my sleeve, "please don't think me ungrateful. I've wanted to thank you for all you did and tried to do, but it wasn't possible. You see, those men would not have understood. Someday I'll explain—"

"Don't bother," I said. "Anybody who'd try to take an old man's ranch away from him doesn't owe me anything, least of all, explanations."

She stiffened up, her face went white, and those

black eyes turned to poison, quick as that. "You are a stupid fool!" she said contemptuously. "I shall explain nothing!"

She turned away from me, and I was just as pleased. I wanted no truck with that black-eyed woman, but the way I saw it, my troubles had only just begun.

About a half-hour later, when I was hungry enough to chew my own boots, they called us to breakfast, and about that time there were horses riding up outside.

One glance through the window sent me stepping back to my room to pick up a gun. It wasn't in me to wear a gun to any man's table, but this here was different. So I taken up a pistol and shoved it down behind my waistband within easy grasp.

Outside there I'd seen Dayton and Oliphant, that city man I'd first seen with Dayton and Dorinda. With them was Nolan Sackett. It was the first time I ever laid eyes on kinfolk of mine when I wasn't pleased.

There were some others, too, and one of them was a wiry, sallow-faced man with the snakiest black eyes you ever did see. He had a tied-down gun which some gunfighters favor, and a way about him that told me he figured himself a handy man with a gun.

When I walked into the dining room Old Ben Mandrin was already settin' up to table, and he looked at me just as perky as could be. "You're walking into trouble, boy," he said. "Are you with me?"

"I reckon we share enemies," I said.

Roderigo came in suddenly, and he glanced quickly at me—doubtfully, I thought, like maybe of a sudden I wasn't to be trusted.

The others showed up at the door.

"Come in! Come in!" Old Ben was smiling and

easy, and it throwed them. I mean they didn't know what to make of him, for without doubt they had come to lay it on the line and tell him the ranch was theirs and he'd have to get off. You could see it in their eyes.

We all sat down to table, and me, I couldn't figure where I stood in all this. Seemed to me I wasn't getting any nearer the gold I'd lost, nor had I any clue as to where it was. And Dorinda wasn't about to tell me, if she knew.

All my life I've been getting myself tangled up where it was none of my affair, and never could figure out why. Maybe it was just that I followed the easiest line, maybe I wanted too much to do things for folks, maybe I was just easily persuaded. Anyway, I was tangled up now.

Right from the start when I saw the black-eyed woman a-settin' there looking at me, a homely man, I knew I was shaping up for trouble. Yet no sooner am I shut of her than I get tangled up with this old man, and from what I'd seen of him he was fit to care for himself. . . . Well, maybe not that night up on the mountain. If I hadn't carried him out of there he'd be waitin' for buzzards by now. But with a tough old man like that, you can't be sure.

This Dayton was a rugged man in his own way, but all polish and surface. I didn't take to him. But now he'd brought me face to face with my kin.

Nolan Sackett came in a step or two behind him, and we looked at each other across the room.

"You could be in better company," I said, right off.

He grinned at me. "Show's on you," he said. "You're one of those preachin' Sacketts."

He was as broad in the shoulders as I, and a right powerful man, maybe twenty pounds heavier, with a big chest and thick arms that swelled out his shirt sleeves until they were like to bust. His face was wider than mine, with a blunt jaw and a nose that had been broken sometime back, but he had the Sackett look to him, all right, and all we Sacketts favor, more or less.

"I never drew a gun on no Sackett," I said, "and I hope you don't fix it so's I have to."

"You could leave out of here," he said. He had a tough, insolent way about him, but he was curious, too, for here we kinfolk had met up away out in California, a far piece from the Tennessee mountains.

"You finally clean out them Higginses?" he asked.

"Tyrel fetched the last one."

"They were fighters. I mind the time two of them had me cornered up on McLean Rock, and me with a bullet in me."

"Was that you? My brother Orrin told me of it. He toted you down off the mountain, piggy-back. Ten, twelve miles."

Dayton was irritated. "We came on business, Nolan. In case you've forgotten."

Nolan ignored him. "Rose Marie Higgins came around on mule back . . . one of the Trelawney girls with her. She came to find where those Higginses were so's they could have Christian burial."

"Orrin, he went back up and dug for them both," I said, "and he spoke words over them, and read from the Book. Then he wrote them—their people, that is. He wrote them to tell where the graves were.

"Given time," I said, "we Smoky Mountain and Cumberland Sacketts always bury our dead, we bury them Christian."

"Like out on the Mojave?" Nolan said, wicked-like.

"Wasn't much time," I explained, "and I had a

woman with me. Had there been time, I'd have read over them."

"Nolan . . . " Dayton was getting almight upset over our talk.

"You came on business," Nolan said, "so get on with it."

"It concerns you!" Dayton declared angrily. "If anything goes wrong . . ."

"I know," Nolan said patiently, "if anything goes wrong I've got to do the fightin.' That's what I'm paid for. All right, you settle your affairs, and when fightin' time comes around, I'll be there."

"I hope you ain't," I said. "I never read over no Sackett, and I ain't honin' to."

"You tell me where at you keep the Book," Nolan said. "I'll be doin' the readin.'"

"Come, come, gentlemen!" Old Ben, he looked as cheerful as a 'possum eatin' persimmons. "No business until after we've eaten."

"I hate to spoil your appetite, old man," Dayton said, in that nasty way he had, "but I came to foreclose. I own this ranch."

Glancing across the table, I happened to notice Dorinda. She was looking at those raw, chewed-out hands of Old Ben's like she couldn't believe what she saw.

"Your hands, Mr. Mandrin! You've hurt your hands!"

seven

For a minute there, the room was as empty of sound as if everybody had suddenly lost their voices, even their power to breathe. Old Ben Mandrin, supposedly moving only from his bed to a chair and back again, had the palms of his hands raked and lacerated like nothing you ever saw. They weren't bandaged . . . there was no real need of that, but they were raw and plenty sore.

The question in everybody's mind but mine was, how did they get that way? And the old coot was enjoying it. Why, I don't think he'd had so much fun since the last time he made somebody walk the plank . . . if he ever did.

Dayton was studying him, his eyes hot with suspicion, and Oliphant was almighty worried. Nolan Sackett, he just threw a hard look at Old Ben's hands, then at his face, and then Nolan went to eating.

Old Ben gestured carelessly. "It's nothing, Dorinda, don't worry your mind about it."

He looked too self-satisfied to please Dayton. By all Dayton's figuring, the old man should be worried sick and begging for a way out, but there he sat, all smug and smart, those old devil eyes of his brighter than a raccoon's.

Old Ben tied into his food like he'd earned it, and there for a while nobody had anything to say. Me, I was fair-to-middlin' hungry, but most of all what I needed was sleep. There'd been none the night before, and very little for some time past, and it was going to do my eye and my shooting no good, if it came to that.

When Old Ben sat back to enjoy his coffee he said, "Old man my age doesn't have many pleasures, and what he has he figures to pay for.

"When Dorinda here started being nice to me, and seemed to set her cap for me, I knew something was in the wind. Turner had introduced her to me as his niece, but Turner had never mentioned a niece before, and when she started offering to care for me and the like, I was suspicious.

"Then when Turner asked me for a loan to keep his bank afloat, I gave some thought to it. He'd loaned me cash a time or two a long while back . . . or rather, his father had, and I owed the bank some help.

"Meanwhile, Dorinda was still around the place, fetching and carrying for me of her own free will, making me more comfortable, fixing the blanket over my knees, putting a pillow back of my head, and moving about the place, swishing her skirts.

"Think that doesn't do a lot for an old man? It did for me. Now, I had no fancy in my mind that she was starting to care for me. Maybe when I was fifty, or even a mite later, but not now; but I could still enjoy her being there and watching her move around.

"You've got to admit she's pretty much of a woman, and she was always the lady. But you've got to admit she keeps what she's got so you know it's there."

He chuckled. "I reckon I'll miss her."

"Get to the point," Dayton said. "I want you out of here . . . today."

That Dayton now . . . he was a man I could come to dislike.

Old Ben's eyes turned on Dayton like a pair of six-shooters, and he said, "You are to be disappointed, Mr. Dayton. I am not leaving. You are not taking my property, which is worth fifty times that note I signed for Turner, and which you now hold. You are not taking my property now . . . or ever."

He had changed so sudden it startled a body. Here he was—or seemed to be—a doddering old man talking about a young woman . . . and then his tone changed and those old eyes of his changed, and Dayton knew right away that he was facing into trouble.

"What do you mean?" Dayton leaned forward. "Why, you damned old fool! That note's due and you know it, and I'm granting you no time. Every friend you have who might lend you money is in as bad shape as you are because of this drought! Now you get off this ranch, and get off now!"

That Ben Mandrin was a hard old man. He chuckled, one of the meanest chuckles you ever heard, and he said, "Why, Mr. Dayton, I'm going to surprise you. I'm going to pay you your petty little note . . . with interest!"

He reached down under the table, and from between his knees, which had been covered by his blanket, he took a sack that he set out on the table in front of all of us.

"There it is, Mr. Dayton, figured down to the last penny . . . and in gold."

When he set that sack down there in the middle

103

of the table we all heard the chink of coins, but Dayton couldn't believe it. He grabbed that sack and jerked it open, spilling those gold coins out on the cloth.

They were gold, all right, and enough to pay off that note, that paltry little sum for which Dayton and Oliphant planned to steal more than a hundred thousand acres of land in one of the loveliest places a body could find.

No, Dayton couldn't believe it. He wouldn't believe it. He knew Old Ben was out of cash. He knew nobody around could afford to loan him money. In his own mind he had already owned the ranch and was thinking of how he could advertise back east and start selling it off, as others were doing.

That black-eyed witch woman looked at the gold, and then she looked across the table at Dayton, and those black eyes were pure poison. "So now, Mr. Dayton," she said coldly, "where do we go from here?"

Roderigo looked as surprised as any of them; only Nolan Sackett seemed to take it without any excitement. He just looked over at Old Ben and said, "All right if I finish eatin' before I go?"

"By all means," the old devil said. "Please enjoy yourselves. After all"—and he sounded mighty sarcastic—"you are my guests."

The gold lay right there on the table where it had spilled, and Roderigo couldn't seem to take his eyes from it. Nolan Sackett ate with good appetite, but the others, including that sallow devil with the black eyes, hadn't much taste for eating. Dayton started several times to speak, but each time he gave it up, for there was just nothing he could say.

Finally, Old Ben spoke up. "You have tasted my hospitality"—his voice was dry, but there was a cutting edge to it—"now *get out!* And you, Dayton

. . . if you ever show up on my property again, for any reason whatsoever, I shall have you horse-whipped!"

Dayton almost staggered when he got to his feet, for he was a whipped man already, and it showed. Oliphant got up and, more leisurely, so did the black-eyed gunman and Nolan himself.

Dayton looked over at Dorinda. "You coming?"

"Do you take me for a fool?" Oh, she was beautiful, all right, but she had a wicked tongue. "I left you before because I knew you were a tin-horn, and you brought me back by force. If you ever try it again, I'll kill you myself!"

Old Ben chuckled, and Dayton went white as a man can get and still live, then he ducked out of the door.

Nolan Sackett leaned over the table and scooped up the gold and swept it into the sack. "Dayton," he called, "you forgot somethin'!"

Nolan paused, filling the door with his bulk. He hefted the sack in his hand, and then he turned back and looked at Old Ben. "Now, I wonder," he said, kind of musing out loud, "where would a man get this kind of gold? Minted gold, and quite a lot of it, some of it old, mighty old."

He put on his hat. "This I got to contemplate . . . I got to contemplate." And he stepped outside and closed the door behind him.

Old Ben was clutching the edge of the table with both hands. Some of the abrasions and cuts had opened and there was blood on the edge of the white cloth.

"Kill him!" he said. "Sackett . . . *kill him!*"

I stared at him, and then I said, "I've got no call to kill him."

"You damned fool!" Old Ben shouted. "Kill him, I say!"

Nobody moved, and Old Ben's face turned dark with angry blood, his eyes glared, and for a minute there I thought he'd have a stroke.

"That man," he said, "will be the death of some of us. Remember what I say."

"Not me," I replied. "I've nothing at stake here."

He looked at me as if he had seen me for the first time. "Yes . . . of course. I had forgotten that."

Nobody made any comment, but I guess we were all figuring on the amount of unfinished business there was at that table. Dorinda Robiseau was suddenly on her own, but with no expectations of money like she'd had, having been promised part of this deal.

Old Ben Mandrin, whom I'd admired for his guts, suddenly began to look like a mighty mean, cantakerous, evil old man. He had saved his ranch, but he had Nolan Sackett to worry about; for however you looked at it, there had been a pretty definite threat in what Nolan said.

Nolan Sackett knew, as anybody would, that such gold had to come from somewhere. Old Ben had apparently been broke. Turner had assured Dayton that this was so. Roderigo, his own grandson, had believed him broke. Then Old Ben shows up with a sack full of minted gold and pays off his debt.

Where had the gold come from?

About that time I suddenly began to look at my hole card. And it was well that I did.

The old man had gotten that gold—of which the amount he'd paid to Dayton was only a small part —on his middle-of-the-night ride with me. When he left me on that pass and turned off along the ridge, he had gone to that gold.

Was this all of it? Or was there more?

Pushing back from the table, I got up and went to my room where, I got out my gear. Something told me to get out of this house, and I wanted to . . . badly.

Roderigo followed me as I carried my gear out and dumped it on the edge of the veranda. "You're leaving?" he asked.

"Yes."

"My grandfather wishes to see you. He said he had promised you mules."

So he had . . . and I was going to need those mules. "All right," I said, and we walked back inside.

He still sat at the table, although in just the few minutes I had been gone it had been cleared. He looked tired now, and I couldn't wonder at it after all he had gone through. He had let down now, and the weariness of that long ride and the crawling among the rocks was getting to him. For the first time since I had met him, he looked his years.

"You helped me," he said when Roderigo had gone from the room, "when there was nobody else I dared call on. I'm having them drive in some mules, and I shall make you a present of twenty."

"That's a lot of mules."

He shrugged. "There are several hundred on the place. There are over six thousand head of cattle here or elsewhere that I own, and nearly a thousand horses. It is a small payment for what I owe you. Besides"—and a little of the Old Ben flashed into his eyes—"it will lighten the load on my range. Unless it rains, and rains well before summer sets in, I'll lose a good many head of stock."

He scratched out a bill of sale for the mules and passed it across the table. "Roderigo knows of this. It will be all right."

Then he hitched around in his chair and looked up at me. "Did the sight of that gold make you less of an honest man?"

"I can't see that having gold has bought you very much."

He grunted. "All this? What do you call this?"

"How many people can you trust? When you were in trouble you had to reach out for a stranger to help you."

"Maybe I was a fool to do that."

"That's your problem." I folded the bill of sale and put it in my shirt pocket. "What are you going to do about *her?*"

"Can't cage an eagle, boy. She'll have to go. I could keep her here and give her anything she wanted, and soon she'd start to hate me because she'd be tied to me. You make bars of gold and an eagle will bite at them, trying to get out."

"You can see she doesn't leave here broke. Hell of a thing, for a woman to be broke."

He swung around in his chair. "You're too damned sentimental, Sackett. It'll get you nowhere. Still, if you're hunting a job you can have one here. I'll give you a working share."

"No."

"You turn down a million dollars awful easy, boy. This ranch will be worth it. You'll live to see it. Is it so easy to turn down a lot of money?"

I just looked at him, and buttoned up that pocket that held twenty mules. "Mister," I said roughly, "I could have had it last night, up there on the mountain. I could have rolled you off that cliff and come back and turned in . . . nobody would have known the difference."

"Thought of it, did you?"

"No . . . but look at it yourself."

"But you brought me back." He looked up at me, those hard old eyes appraising me. "That's why I need you here. I need an honest man."

"What about Roderigo?"

He snorted. "He's honest enough, I think, and he'd try. But he's weak . . . he's a gentleman. He would try to fight clean, and he'd lose. You'd fight them the way they'd fight you, and you'd win."

"Good-bye, Ben Mandrin," I answered him.

I walked to the door and stood there a moment, looking back at him. He had that blanket over his knees and he kept one hand under the blanket, and I wasn't going to turn my back on a man like that.

"I hope you got all you wanted last night," I said. "Nolan Sackett or somebody in that crowd could track a squirrel across a flat rock."

"So can you," he said. "So can you."

I stepped out of that door backwards . . . after one quick look to be sure the yard was empty.

eight

She was standing near the corral when I walked out
there, a rarely beautiful woman, with her black eyes
and red lips, ànd that way she had of moving and
looking at a man.

She was wearing a dark red dress that really stood
out against that old pole corral, and it looked to me
like she had fixed herself up kind of special. So right
away I began to wonder what it was she was after.

"No one else could have done it," she said. "It
had to be you." She put her hand on my sleeve.
"Thank you for helping him."

That was sort of a leading statement, so I just
said, "Ma'am, I've got to saddle my horse. They're
rounding up some mules for me."

"You're a rare man, Tell Sackett. I wish I had
known you long ago."

"You think it would have made a difference? We'd
have both gone the same ways we have gone."

"What are you going to do?"

"Arizona . . . I'm headed back for the mines."

"Across that awful desert?" She shuddered. "I
hope I shall never see another desert."

"It's the way I've got to go. If there's anything I want, it's back there."

"Is there a girl?"

Well, now, how could I answer that when I didn't know myself? There had been a girl. And then she had gone back east to visit some folks of hers, and when she was due to come back she just didn't come. Nor was there any letter that I ever got. . . .

Ange . . . Ange Kerry.

"No, ma'am," I said, "I don't think there's a girl. Looks to me like I'm a lonesome man riding a lonesome country, and I don't see no end to it."

"There could be, Tell."

Well, sir, I looked down into those big black eyes and saw those moist lips, and thinks I, if this here's a trap, they surely picked the right kind of bait.

"Ma'am," I said, "you're a lot of woman on the outside."

She stiffened up like I'd slapped her. "What do you mean by that?"

"Well, I sure don't cut no figure as a man knowing women, but it seems to me what you wear is a lot of feeling where it shows. I don't think there's very much down inside. I'd be like that old man in there . . . I'd as soon make love to you, ma'am, but I'd want to keep both your hands in sight. I'd never know which one held the knife."

Oh, she was mad! She started as if to slap me, her lips tightening up and her face kind of flattening out with anger. But she held herself in. She was keeping a tight rein on her feelings, and she waited for a moment or two before she replied.

"You're wrong, you know. It's just that I've not found the right man . . . I've had to hold myself in, I've had to be careful. For you I could change. I could be different."

"All right," I said suddenly, "suppose we give it a

try. I'll saddle a horse for you, and you can ride back to Arizona with me. If you still feel the same way by the time we get to Prescott—"

She caught my arm again, stepping up so close I could really fill my nostrils with that sweet-smelling stuff she wore. "Oh, Tell, just take me with you! I mean it! I'll do *anything!* I'll love you like you've never been loved! I'll even go into the desert with you. I'll ride all the way to Dallas if you suggest it."

Then Roderigo rode back in with two vaqueros and they had my mules. I'll give him this—he had gone along to be sure they were the best, and they were. Every mule of them was good . . . I'd go a long way to find their equal. These were not the little Spanish mules, but big ones from Missouri, valuable animals on the frontier.

"If you like, we will hold them, señor, then they will be no expense until you are prepared to load them and go."

"I'd be obliged."

He stood there, fidgeting around while I saddled up the stallion and made ready to start for town.

"Be careful," he said, "in riding across La Nopalera. Men have been killed from ambush there."

"*Gracias.*"

One last thing he had to tell me before I rode out. He came up to me as I gathered the reins and reached for the saddle horn.

"The man who was here—the slight one with the black eyes?"

"Yes."

"He was a partner . . . a friend. That one was on the desert also, and he is the one who knows of your gold, *amigo.* I have it from them." He jerked his head to indicate the vaqueros. "There are few secrets, señor, if one listens well."

"Do you know his name?"

113

"Dyer . . . Sandeman Dyer."

I knew that name . . . from long ago. It stirred memories that brought with them a smell of gun-smoke and wet leather. . . .

Why is it that smells are so strongly associated with memories? But it is usually the smell that in-spires the recall of the memory, and not the other way, as happened to me now.

"Do you know him?" Roderigo asked.

"Maybe . . . I'm not sure."

"Be careful, señor. It is said that he is a very dangerous man . . . and he has many friends. He rode in from the north some weeks ago, and twenty men rode with him. There have been raids and robberies since—nobody knows for sure, but it is believed that he is the one who leads them.

"He is a gunman, señor, very dangerous. He has killed a man in Virginia City, and another in Pioche of whom we knew."

So I swung into the saddle and looked down at my big hands resting on the pommel, work-hardened hands, used to pick handle, shovel, axe, and rope. And to guns also.

"It does not matter, amigo. If he has the gold that is mine, and that also which belongs to my friends, I shall ask him for it."

"You wish to die?"

"Nobody wishes to die."

So I turned the stallion and rode away from the ranch, and toward the pueblo.

All that remained now was to get my gold, and the man to see was Sandeman Dyer. Or . . . was I too suspicious? Was this a trap? Had the information been planted, in hopes that it would reach me?

It was dark when I came again to the pueblo of Los Angeles, and there were lights in many homes and other buildings. I came into town by the old *brea* pits road, and left my horse at the town's best livery stable. And so I returned to the Pico House, and my room there.

A man with a flat-brimmed white hat sat in the lobby reading the *Star*. He looked at me over the edge of the paper, only his eyes showing between paper and hat brim.

My few things were in my room, to which I added my rifle and the gear recovered with my horses. Only the gold was gone now.

I was tired . . . bone-weary. I felt as if I had been drugged. Tonight I should search out Sandeman Dyer, but I was too tired. Tonight I would rest, at last, in a bed.

I peeled off my shirt, and filled the basin with water and washed, then combed my hair. Standing before the mirror I looked at myself, seeing the old scars, marks of old wounds from gun battles and from the war, and here or there the finer, thinner scars of knife wounds. Those scars showed me how lucky I had been.

It was not in me to believe myself fated to die at any given time. Deep within me I knew, having seen many men die, that no man is immune to death at any time at all. During every moment, walking or sleeping, we are vulnerable . . . I could die tonight . . . tomorrow.

Young men do not like to believe that. Each has within him that little something that says: Others may die, but not me, not me. I shall live.

Despite all those who die around him, this is what he believes. But I did not believe it, and I had never believed it from the first moment I saw a good man die, when the evil lived. I could believe in no special providence for any man. Tomorrow, when I went hunting my gold, a bullet or a knife might kill me.

But it was not in me to refrain from going. Nor

could I call this bravery. My determination held none of that. It was simply because it was in me to go. I had never learned how to hang back from what it was up to me to do.

Sitting down on the bed, I reached for a dusty boot. One hand upon the toe, the other on the heel, I waited, just a moment longer. Weariness made me sag inwardly, made me cringe at the sound of footsteps in the hall outside my door.

After a moment there was a light tap on the door and, stepping across to the door's side, my hand on my gun, I asked, "Who is it?"

"A letter for you, sir. It arrived yesterday, but I expected to see you at the desk."

"Slip it under the door."

There was a moment's hesitation, and then the letter appeared. It was addressed in a flowing masculine hand, one I had never seen before.

Ripping open the brown envelope, I found a sealed letter within, and with it a short note. I read the note first.

Mr. Sackett,
Dear Sir:
    When the mail from the stage you saw wrecked in the canyon was brought to us it was found to contain this letter to you, addressed in care of me. As it may be of importance, I am sending it forward.

                                    Hardy.

Then I opened the letter, and when I unfolded the closely written pages, I saw that it was from Ange.

Dropping upon the bed, I read it through, which I could do with a bit of work, for I'd little enough time at school in my boyhood, and read but slowly.

She had been ill. . . . She was well. . . . Did I wish

her to come back? And then almost in the next sentence . . . she was coming back. She would take the first stage. She would meet me in Prescott.

I folded up the letter and thrust it into my pants pocket. Then I pulled the pants off and got into bed. Drawing the blankets up, I stretched out carefully, for the bed was made for a shorter sleeper than I, and slowly I let my long body relax against the comfort of the mattress.

Ange . . . my own Ange . . . Ange was coming west. She would meet me in Prescott.

Then I sat bolt upright.

Ange would meet me in Prescott, where I would be arriving with another woman!

Presently I lay back on the bed and tried to relax once more, but no matter how I tried . . .

Suddenly, I was wide awake. Somehow I had fallen asleep, but something, some faint noise, had awakened me in spite of my exhaustion. Starting to move, I caught myself in time. Somebody was in the room.

The door was closed. The window was open the merest crack, yet somebody was inside the room.

A faint creak told me that whoever it was stood right beside the bed. Through the slit of a scarcely opened eye I saw the loom of a dark figure, the faint gleam of light on a knife blade, and I threw myself against him, knocking him back to the floor.

Choking with fear and fury, I rolled on top of him and grabbed at his knife wrist, bending it sharply back toward the floor. I grabbed him by the belt with the other hand and heaved myself up, lifting him with me, and swung him bodily at the window.

With a tremendous crash of glass he went through it and I heard a wild, despairing yell, then the thud as he struck in the street below.

The door, I then noticed, was ever so slightly ajar.

Pushing it shut, I shot the bolt and went back to bed. Cold night air blew through the broken window. Vaguely I heard excited talk in the street below ... but I decided I wasn't interested.

Presently heavy boots rushed up the hall and there was a frenzied knocking at my door.

Lifting my head, I said, "Damn it, go away! Can't a man sleep around here?"

Somebody started to reply, and I added, "If I have to get out of bed again, somebody else goes into the street. Now you goin' to leave me be?"

There was a subdued murmur, then quiet footsteps going off down the hall. I pulled the blankets around me, and in a few minutes I was asleep.

It was broad daylight when I woke up. Sunlight was streaming in through the broken window, and I got out of bed. Still a mite foggy from the heavy sleep, I went to the basin, washed, and dressed. When I had pulled on my shirt I looked out of the window, but there was nothing in the street to show where anybody had fallen.

Now one thought and one only was in my mind. Today I was going to see Sandeman Dyer.

When I came down the steps it looked like everybody was waiting for me. The manager of the hotel —leastways I figured it to be him—came up and told me I'd have to pay for breaking the window.

"Breaking the window? Mister, I broke no window. I didn't even touch it. If you want to get paid, you find the man who went through it. You collect from him."

He started to argue, and I said, "Look, mister, I don't like to get mad. Last night was once, and far's I can see, that's enough. Maybe I should point out that you got bigger windows down here."

Well, he kind of drew back, but I stepped right after him. "Also, you might spend some of the time you seem to have to waste after me and find out how that thief had a key . . . and he had one. You in the habit of givin' keys to thieves?"

I'd spoken loud, and several of the folks standing about moved closer to listen. That man began to worry.

"Ssh!" he said. He was all of a flutter to get shut of me now. "Forget it. I am afraid I was mistaken." And he hurried off.

I turned then to look at those people around me and I said, "Anybody here know where I can find a man named Dyer? Sandeman Dyer?"

Nobody seemed to know a thing. You never saw such vague folks in your born days. Everybody had been interested up to that point, and then nobody was. In less than two minutes after I spoke that name the lobby was empty.

I went outside, where sunlight lay on the dusty street and upon the walks. Pausing on the corner, I looked across the Plaza in the direction of Sonora town . . . an unlikely place to look for Dyer.

Closer to me was the Calle de los Negros, better known as Nigger Alley, and Tao's gambling house.

Taking my time, I strolled here and there about the town, looking into store windows and watching the horse cars. Most of them seemed to be going out Spring Street to a place called Washington Gardens.

On the streets the folks themselves were a sight to behold, and when it came to the Californios themselves, you never saw such a dressed-up lot of folks. Many wore short jackets of silk, figured calico, or beaded buckskin, white linen shirts open at the neck, black silk handkerchiefs knotted loosely around the neck, and pants of velveteen or broadcloth, or sometimes of beautifully tanned white buckskin, and nearly every one wore a silk sash, usually bright red. The serapes ranged from Indian blankets to fine broadcloth.

The handsome outfits these men had, made me look a poor mountain boy, even in my new twelve-dollar suit. Why, I fancy it must have taken a thousand dollars or more to get some of them dressed. And their saddles and bridles! You never saw so much silver. And two-thirds of them, I was sure, with dirt floors in their houses.

Here and there you still saw men with long hair, and some of them with it not just to their shoulders. In some cases it was braided. The younger ones had taken to trimming their hair, Anglo fashion, but not all of them.

Everywhere a body looked there were black-eyed señoritas, flirting with you with quick, teasing glances that made the red climb right up a man's neck. Me, I already had two women on my hands, when I wasn't fairly used to one, and more trouble shaping up than you could shake a stick at.

As I went about the town, everybody I asked about Sandeman Dyer was warning me about him. But I was more fearful of what would happen when I rode into Prescott with that black-eyed witch girl and found Ange a-waiting for me than I was of what was ahead of me right now. Ange was a red-haired girl, and she was one with a mind of her own, and she'd had will enough to survive in the high-up mountains of Colorado before I found her there.*

Suddenly a rider turned into Main Street from Spring, and I saw it was that black-eyed gunman who had been at Old Ben's ranch. He rode past, not noticing me, heading for the Calle de los Negros. He would be going to Dyer, I could lay a bet on it.

*Sackett, Bantam Books, 1961.

But just as I turned to follow, a voice spoke behind me. "You take my advice and you'll leave Dyer alone."

It was Nolan Sackett.

We stood there facing each other in the street, two mighty big men, both of us armed, and both carrying the scars we'd picked up since we left Tennessee, and a few from before that.

"If he's a friend of yours, you just tell him to hand over my gold. I got no quarrel with him."

Nolan didn't even smile. "Don't be a fool, man! You came out of that alive, and you're damned lucky. Now let well enough alone."

"I'm going after my gold."

He looked disgusted and mad all to once. "Look," he said irritably, "you're kin of mine, or I'd let you go your way and get killed. Dyer has forty men around him, and he himself is one of the most dangerous men alive."

"So he sends a man to knife me in the dark?"

Nolan had an odd look in his eyes. "Believe me, Tell, that man never came from Dyer. Dyer just couldn't care less about you."

He shoved his hat back on his head, and there was a worried look in his eyes. "For a man who says he minds his own affairs, you can pick up trouble faster than anybody I ever did see. You'd be right smart if you just climbed up on that stallion of yours and lit out for the high-up desert. There's three or four passels of folks here just a-honin' to see you dead and buried."

"You tell Dyer to have my gold ready. You go right along and tell him."

"Damn it, if you come against him you'll be facing me. I'm with him."

"Like I say, I never drew iron on ary a Sackett, but if you stand between me and what's rightfully mine they can bury you along with Sandeman Dyer."

"There'll be forty men, damn you!"

"Seems to me Dyer can't be too sure of himself if he needs all that company. You go stand beside him, Nolan, and when they bury me they can dig the grave wide enough for the lot of us."

When he had gone I stood there on the street, staring off toward the hills. Maybe I was crazy. After all, why not get into the saddle and ride away? Most of that gold was my own . . . and true, it represented my stake for the future. It represented the cattle I wanted to buy to stock a ranch in Arizona. It represented a future for Ange and me, if future there was to be.

And those other folks who lost gold entrusted to me . . . they could less afford to lose their gold than I could, although they would not lose near so much.

Nobody needed to tell me what I'd be going into, and I had no plan, no idea of what to do. Like I said, I never was much account at plotting or planning or working things out. All I know is to go bulling in and do whatever comes natural. Only thing I regretted was Nolan Sackett being there.

It went against me to fire on a Sackett of the blood. It would go hard to take lead from him, or to shoot him down where he stood. Even a Clinch Mountain Sackett was kin, and I wanted no shooting between us. Still, he had chosen his side, and now it was up to me.

Odd thing, the way a man is. Trouble waited me there, I knew, maybe injury and death, but I turned around and started down the street, and headed right into it. Maybe I just didn't know any better.

Pausing on the corner, I taken out my six-shooter and spun the cylinder. She worked smooth and easy.

A passerby gave me a sharp glance and hurried on past.

That man who took one look and hurried on was the smart one. He saw trouble and avoided it. Only he didn't have all that gold awaiting him.

Tao's place was sure jumping. I mean, there were a lot of folks there, all of them gambling or drinking. By the time I reached the bar they had me spotted. Until that moment I'd have sworn I didn't know any but one or two of the men who had followed me out on the Mojave, but right away I recognized two of them here.

That black-eyed gunman was standing at the bar when I walked up to it, and he had a taunting, challenging sort of look to him that riled me. "You tell Dyer," I said, "that Tell Sackett is here, and wants to see him."

"He knows you're here."

Two men had walked over to a table near the door, where they sat down. Two other men strolled up to a card game and stood by, watching the play. A man playing at that table glanced around thoughtfully, then laid down his hand and cashed in his chips. He got up, kind of careless-like, and went out the door. He was a wise one . . . he knew enough to get out before things busted wide open.

Nobody needed to tell me, after all, where to find Sandeman Dyer. The minute I saw him, I knew him.

He was sitting at a table in a little alcove, a man of less than medium height, with square shoulders, and a kind of angular face with high cheekbones. When a body first laid eyes on him it seemed that his face was out of kilter somehow, that maybe it was misshaped, but you couldn't find any one thing about it that was wrong by itself. It was just an impression you got.

He was smiling now, smiling easy and friendly.

And then I thought back to Shiloh, and I felt reason to worry, for when this man smiled he was dangerous indeed.

"Well, now, Sackett, it has been a long time. A very long time." And he held out his hand to me.

When I took it I knew how it would feel . . . cold, and clammy. For I had shaken this man's hand before, and it meant no more now than it did then. He was a great one for shaking hands. I didn't make the mistake of forgetting his little tricks; only knowing Dyer, I knew it would not be now.

Sandeman Dyer—we called him Sandy then—was a talker. He was a man with a love for the sound of his own voice. He was not only a talker, but a man who liked to parade what he knew, and he was almighty sure that he knew a whole lot more than anybody else. That easy smile of his, that easy laugh, they sort of covered the contempt he felt for anybody and everybody.

He was a bright man, all right, and a shrewd one. He was cunning like an animal . . . it was a savage cunning . . . but when the Good Lord put him together something went wrong. For he was a man without mercy, a man with cruelty so deeply ingrained in him that it was the most important part of his life. He was made up of cruelty and self-importance, I guess, in about equal amounts.

Yes, he loved to talk, to parade his smartness, but the trouble was he could stop talking awful sudden. . . . He could break off in the middle of a sentence and kill you, or have you killed.

I'd seen it happen, for back there at Shiloh we were in the same outfit. The first time I saw it happen—the first time he shot an unarmed prisoner—I thought he'd gone wild from the pounding of the guns. Cruelty was a rare thing in the war. Fireside folks who talk about war and read about it, they figure it's cruel more often than not, but it simply isn't so. When you kill in war it is usually impersonal, except when you've seen a friend shot down, and then you strike back and hard . . . if you can.

You kill in war because it is your job, and because you want to survive, and not because of any desire to kill. Cruelty takes time, and there is mighty little of that in war. But Sandy Dyer was a different kettle of fish.

The second time it was a major we'd captured, a handsome man of thirty-five, a gallant gentleman, who when trapped had surrendered. Come right down to it, he was *my* prisoner. That was what made me mad. But when Dyer started talking to him nice and friendly like, I thought nothing of it. There were six of us there, and the prisoner. But mighty soon that talk of Dyer's began to take on a nasty edge I didn't care much for, and I said so. He paid me no mind.

"Got a family, Major?" Dyer asked, ever so gentle.

"Yes. I have a wife and two sons."

"Those boys, now. They in the army?"

"They are too young, sir. One is six and one is twelve."

"Ah . . ." He looked up, innocent as a baby, and he looked right into that major's eyes and he said, "I wonder how many times your wife has been raped since this war started?"

It came so sudden we all sort of jumped, and three, four of us, we started to bust in. That major's face had gone white and he stepped forward and drew back his hand to strike, and Dyer stepped back out of reach and he said, "Major . . . you ain't never going to know."

Well, I'd heard of men getting a gun out fast, but I'd never seen it. In the high-up mountains it was mostly rifles we used, and the repeating pistol was scarce twenty-odd years old, and mighty few of us had even seen one.

He just drew that pistol and shot that major right in the belly.

Me, I knocked him down.

He hit ground all in a heap and then he went sort of crazy. Rightly speaking, I expect he was crazy all the time. Later on, when the story was told around I began to hear of other things he'd done. Anyway, he came off the ground and rushed at me, and I hit him again.

There was trouble over that, and a sort of drumhead court-martial and he was discharged out of the service. I heard afterward he'd joined Quantrill or Bloody Bill Anderson or one of those.

And now here he was, facing me across the table, and I knew he hadn't forgotten those times I'd hit him. I also knew he was dangerous as a cornered rattler and would strike, like a rattler in the "blind," without warning.

He was no rational man, and those others with him, they would do what he said.

Under my shirt I could feel cold sweat on my body, and I was scared. This here was a man I'd hoped never to see again, and I had walked right into him. Only I had one advantage over the others he might have tangled with. I knew that when he started talking soft and easy, I'd have to be careful.

Another thing I knew. Before we parted one of us was going to die. There just couldn't be any other way.

"Thought you were an eastern man, Dyer," I said. Drawing back a chair, I sat down, but where none of them could get behind me without my seeing them. "I didn't expect to run into you out here."

"I don't expect you wanted to see me, did you, Sackett?"

"Why not?" I said carelessly. Then I added, "I hear one of your boys was good enough to bring my gold in off the desert. I take that kindly."

He smiled, and this time there was something like real humor in the smile. I could see he liked my way of putting it.

"I believe there was some mention of gold," he said, "but I understand it was found on the desert. I had no idea it belonged to you." He went on smiling at me. "I suppose you can identify it?"

Now I could see he was taunting me, being sure there was no way of identifying raw gold, but in that he was wrong. Truth was, I knew mighty little about such things, only what a body hears talking with miners and prospectors, but he didn't have to know that.

"Matter of fact," I said, "I *can* identify it. So can any good assayer. The amount of silver and other mineral associated with gold varies from place to place."

He didn't like that. Not so much because he thought I could identify the gold, as because he hadn't known this fact.

Sitting there, casual like and easy on the surface, I was doing some fast figuring. This was an unbalanced man, deadly fast with a six-shooter, and with a hair-trigger temper. A normal man can be understood to some extent; but this man, though shrewd and calculating up to a point, was apt to do some damned fool thing—some damned deadly thing —on a momentary whim. It was like sitting on a keg of dynamite with a wet fuse. You knew it was going to go, but you didn't know when.

The men he had with him were bandits, adventurers, drifters, men out to make easy money, or money that sounded easy, and they followed him because he had brains and daring, and because they feared to cross him. He had come south hunting money and trouble, and they were with him all the way.

The chances were that most of those men were good with guns. Some were renegades left over from the War Between the States, others were just outlaws he'd picked up.

The way to whip a man is to keep him off-balance, and it seemed to me my best chance to get out of this alive, or with a shooting chance, was to keep him from thinking about it.

"'Member that time we met that outfit of Gray-backs on Owl Creek?" I said. Glancing across the table at the others, I went on, "I never saw the like. Dyer here was on my left. There were six of us moving up to the creek in the late evening. It was coming up to dark, and it was still . . . so still you could hear our clothes rustling as we walked.

"Dyer, he had himself a pair of Remington .36-calibre six-shooters that he spent a good part of his time polishing up. He had those guns belted on, and we all carried rifles.

"Well, sir, we were a-walking along, moving like a pack of Mescaleros, when suddenly we stepped into a clearing. And just as we done so, a party of Rebs came in from the other side, at least twenty in the outfit.

"They were as surprised as we were, only Dyer here, he acted quicker'n you could say scat. He dropped his rifle where he stood and outs with those Remingtons . . . you never heard such fire. You'd have thought he had him one of those Smith-Percival magazine pistols that fire forty shots.

"He just opened up and went to blasting with both guns at once, and that whole party cut and run . . . why, I don't think ary of us got off a shot, only Dyer. He downed three of them, wounded I don't know how many."

Folks somehow have a feeling when something is about to happen, and you'd be surprised how business had fallen off in just those few minutes since I came in. That first man who cashed in his chips, he began it. Maybe a dozen had drifted out since then.

But Sandeman Dyer was a man who liked to hear himself talked about. He sat back and ordered drinks, and we started talking up old times. Yet all the time I was realizing that the fewer outsiders were in that place, the less chance I'd have. Not that Dyer would care much for witnesses. When it came on him to kill, nothing in the world was going to stop him . . . it was a kind of madness.

The worst of it was, he was fast.

Was I quicker with a gun? I surely didn't know. The fact of the matter was, it wouldn't make an awful lot of difference, because when the shooting started, if he didn't get me the rest of them would. Only I made up my mind that no matter how much lead I took, I was going to keep shooting long enough to take him with me. For if ever a man needed to die, it was Sandeman Dyer.

So we talked the afternoon away, and finally I knew I had to let go of the bull.

What I mean is, I had a bull by the tail and I was safe as long as I hung on; but I had to let go sometime, and it was better to pick my own time than to wait until he got impatient.

So finally I said, "Well, it's been friendly, seeing you after all these years, but I've got to start back for Arizona. If you'll hand over my gold, I'll leave out of here."

His expression changed ever so little, his lids flickering just an instant as he adjusted to what I'd said. Our talk had kind of lulled everybody else into quiet. They were kind of scattered out, busy with their own activities, drinking, talking, sure there'd be no trouble.

They didn't know Dyer like I did.

"Why, sure!" He smiled at me with all the warmth of a hungry wolf. "I intended you to have it all the time." He turned his head to the man behind the bar. "Joe, open the safe and bring that sack of gold over here."

And right then, I knew.

It had to be when I put my hand on that gold . . . or when I reached the door with it.

More than likely it would be the last, for he would want to drag it out. He might shoot me in the back, but it was more probable he'd let me get almost to the door, drawing his gun behind my back, and then he'd speak to me, and when I turned he would let me have it.

In my mind, I counted the steps to the door, and it was far, much too far . . . and once I was out in the open room he'd have a clear shot at me.

Suddenly, I realized something else. The afternoon sunlight was falling through the window over our heads, and when I reached that place in the center of the room or a bit beyond and turned, I'd have the sun's glare in my eyes.

Oh, I'll not say he'd seen it that way from the beginning, although with him you never knew. All this talk, when I thought I was getting him to relax and ease off the tension a mite, all that might have been just waiting until the sun was right.

For Sandeman Dyer knew I could shoot.

He had not spoken loudly, and few had heard him except those standing close by. The idle talk on the other side of the room continued, and I heard Joe close the door of the safe and walk back across the room. He put the gold down in front of Dyer and went back to his bar.

There was no sense in wasting time now. Reaching across the table, I said, "Thanks, Sandy," and picked up the gold . . . with my left hand.

He was smiling, his eyes dancing with that odd light I remembered so well, and I knew he had not missed the left hand . . . or my right hand on the edge of the table.

And then I stood up.

All of them were waiting, expecting some word from him. One word, one move from him, and they'd fill me so full of lead folks would be staking my grave for a lead mine.

Suddenly, turning, I thrust out my hand to him. Instantly, I knew I'd done the wrong thing. I'd had it in mind to hang onto him and walk him to the door with me, but the moment my hand went out, I knew this was when he would want to shoot me. It would please that mocking devil of insanity in him to shoot me with my hand thrust out to shake hands.

He had come to his feet, smooth and easy, and he half reached to take my hand, then dropped it for his gun.

My hand was outstretched . . . too far from my gun, so I just lunged with it to stiff-arm him in the chest, but he stepped back quickly, backing into his chair.

For just an instant it had him off-balance, and I threw my left arm across my face and went crash-through the window into the alley.

Believe me, it was a wild gamble, but I hit the window with a shoulder and went through, falling full length in the alley. As I fell, my hand had grasped my gun butt, so when I hit ground my gun came up with the hammer eared back.

And there he was, broad against the window's light. His gun flamed, but he had expected me to be on my feet and he was geared to shoot high. In almost the same instant that his gun flamed, I let the hammer fall, brought it back and fired again, so fast the two shots had but one thundering sound.

He buckled as if somebody had slugged him in the wind, and his gun went off again, harmlessly, in the air, as his finger tightened convulsively on the trigger.

Leaping to my feet, I spread my legs and shot twice more into his body as he fell back. This was one man I wanted dead.

There was a rush of feet from inside, and then a voice spoke out, stopping them.

"Leave him be." It was Nolan Sackett. "You boys just stand hitched."

Stooping down, I felt around for my sack of gold, and picked it up. Then I went up to the window. Dyer was sprawled dead on the floor, and they were just beginning to realize there was nothing to fight for.

"Any of you boys want a buy into this game?" I said. "The pot's open, and bullets are chips!"

Nobody seemed to be holding high cards, so they stood pat. I said to Nolan, "I'm riding out of here. Want to come along?"

"You go to hell," he said politely.

nine

Sometimes the damned fool things a man does are the ones that save his bacon.

When I had my horses all together I tied lead ropes on them and started out of town, and I wasn't sorry to go. Only one thing bothered me, I'd come this far and hadn't seen the ocean sea.

It was over yonder, not too far out of my trail, so when I was heading west across La Nopalera, the big cactus patch that lay north of the *brea* road, I made up my mind of a sudden. I'd no wish to sleep the night at the Mandrin ranch, so what better than a ride down toward Santa Monica and the sea?

Of a sudden I decided to do it, for I might not come this way again. By such whims can a man's life be saved, as mine was saved that evening.

Turning off, I taken the trail for San Vincente Spring, from which Santa Monica, both the old town and the new, so I'd heard, took their water. It was a long ride, and despite the fact that I kept moving right along, it was nigh to midnight before I got where I could hear the sea.

There was a ranch house on the bluff, about a

133

half mile back from the sea, but I was shy of folks and rode clear of it, although I was near enough that their dog barked at me.

The stars were out and a fresh wind from off the sea felt good against my face. Down at the end of the arroyo was a clump of trees, great big old sycamores, and some brush, but there were too many squatters, to judge by the campfires still going. So I turned north along the shore until I found another canyon. Up that canyon about a quarter of a mile I found a clump of trees with nobody around, and I rode in, unsaddled, and bedded down.

It was sure lucky that nobody followed me all the way out there, for I slept like a hibernating bear until the sun found my face through the leaves.

My stock had made a good thing of it on the grass in the clearing, so I taken my time getting around. My saddlebags were empty of grub, and after a bit I saddled up and rode along the shore to the town.

After stabling my horses, I got me a room at the Santa Monica Hotel, and made a dicker with the manager, a man name of Johnson, to take my gold off my hands for cash money.

When he paid it over to me he gave me a sharp look and said, "You seem to be a nice young man. If I were you I should be very careful, carrying that much money. There are thieves hereabouts."

"You don't say!" I said with astonishment. "Well, thank you kindly. I shall be wary of strangers."

They had a bath house there where folks came to take the baths, and it seemed to me a good soaking couldn't but do me good. Whilst I was in the bath I laid my saddlebags close by and my pistol belt atop them where I could lay hand on the gun mighty easy. Several folks came by and looked at me and then at that gun, and they fought shy of me. They were mostly older men, taking the baths for their rheumatism.

After a good meal I walked around town a little, looking at the schoolhouse, the churches, and the railroad, which had been built out there just a year or so earlier. Some folks were saying this would be the biggest seaport on the west coast . . . at least, the biggest south of San Francisco.

A couple of times I went around to check my horses, and from the livery stable door I studied the town to make sure that nobody was following me, or that any of that Dyer outfit had showed up hunting me.

That night I slept, and slept well, in a hotel bed. I mean I just stretched out and didn't mind it a whole lot when my feet pushed out below the covers. I was sure enough in a bed, and nobody knew where I was. However, I slept with those saddlebags under the covers with me, and a six-shooter too. You might say I was not a trusting man.

Most folks can be trusted up to a point, but it always seemed to me the best thing was not to put temptation in their way. Now that black-eyed witch girl . . . she made a business of temptation. When she was around, temptation was always in the way.

It was noontime when I showed up at that Mandrin ranch.

The way I figured, they'd be expecting me at most any other time, and I'd noticed that during dinner-time when they were inside eating, and right after when they took their siesta, the place was quiet as death.

After I thought that word, I tried to unthink it. Death was riding at my heels these days, and I didn't want to charm it to me by thinking of it.

When a man rides as much country as I have, he gets a feeling for it, and wherever he rides, he looks around to get to know it. So it was that I knew just how to come up to the ranch unseen, and I was in the ranch yard and putting ropes on my mules before anybody came out of the house.

The one who appeared was a dark-eyed man wearing a white hat.

"Howdy," he said. "You'd be Tell Sackett."

"Seems like."

"You stirred a lot of talk yonder in the pueblo. Everybody's been wonderin' what became of you."

"I'm a driftin' man, so I drifted."

He stood there trying to size me up, and as I roped my mules together for better handling, I managed not to turn my back on him, nor to seem like I was thinking of such a thing. With mules fidgeting around the way they do, that was simple enough. All the time I was debating whether I should go inside and say good-bye to the old man.

This man with the white hat had a hurt arm, and he limped a mite, too. There was a cut on his face that might have come from broken glass. He looked like a man who might have been thrown out of a window and rolled down a porch roof before falling off into the street.

When I was ready to go I led my stock around in front of the house and looked over at White Hat.

"You," I said, "let's go in and see Old Ben."

"I seen him," he said, mighty sullen. "He knows me."

"You walk in there," I advised him, "and you walk in ahead of me. Looks to me like you tripped over something too big for you already, so don't take chances on it happening again."

It didn't seem he liked that very much, but he walked in ahead of me. It might have been my suspicious mind that prompted it, but it seemed to

me Old Ben was doing a lot of fussing with his
blanket when I came through the door.

That black-eyed girl came down from her room,
dressed for riding, an Indian girl following her with
some bags and suchlike that a woman feels called
upon to tote around.

"Well, Ben," I said, "this here's good-bye. It's
adios. If you plan to see me again, you'll have to
come to Arizona."

His hard old eyes studied me, and they glinted with
a touch of humor mixed with what might have been
respect. "You killed Sandeman Dyer," he said.
"Everybody allowed it couldn't be done."

"Every man is born with death in him," I said.
"It's only a matter of time."

Dorinda was standing there, and when I looked
at her I saw her eyes were wider than usual, her
cheeks kind of pale. I wondered about that, for she
was a composed sort of girl, who didn't get wrought
up by trifles.

"All right, boy!" Old Ben said. "You have a nice
trip. And thanks . . . thanks for everything. Not
many men would have done what you did, and
without pay."

"Those mules look pretty good," I said, "that's
pay enough for a lot of trouble."

Glancing over at Dorinda, I said, "You ready?"

"Go ahead . . . I want to say good-bye to Ben."

"All right," I said, and turned toward the door.

He was too anxious, that old man was. He had
me dead to rights, but he was too anxious. Here
I'd been ready for trouble for weeks, and expecting
it from everywhere, but in that moment I forgot. But
he was in too much of a hurry.

First thing I knew, there was a *whap* of something
past my ear, the heavy *tunk* as it hit the door jamb,
and the bellow of a gun. Me, I was headed for the

outside and there was nothing keeping me. I went out that door like I had fire in my hip pockets, and I'm not ashamed to confess it.

He fired again, and the bullet just fanned air where I'd been, and then I heard the damnedest job of cussing I've heard in my born days.

Around the corner of the house came White Hat, running full tilt with a rifle in his hands. But when he got where he wanted to be, my six-shooter was looking right down his throat, and I said, "You going to drop that rifle, or am I going to drag what's left of you out in the brush for the buzzards to pick over?"

He was a man of decision who recognized the logic of my argument, and he let go of that rifle as if it was hot.

"Los Angeles is quite a ways off," I told him, "and if you're going to walk it, you'd best get started."

About that time Dorinda came out the door just like nothing had happened, and I helped her into the saddle, keeping those horses between the door and me. That was a mighty sour old man in there, and he was remembering that if anybody in the world knew where his cache of pirate gold was, it was a man named William Tell Sackett.

When we rode off I could hear him yelling for White Hat or somebody, only nobody was coming. They would, after a while, but they were bright folks, and kind of shy of shooting.

Once we were on the trail, it was pleasant to ride beside Dorinda, keeping the mules down the trail ahead of us, talking easy-like with that dark-eyed witch girl.

Not that I was ever much of a hand to talk to women. Back in the mountains where I came from I never was much on talk, and my feet were too big for dancing; but along about midnight when the girls started walking out with their friends, I was usually around and about.

Only Dorinda was easy to talk to. She knew how to lead a man on to talk of himself, and somehow she soon had me talking of the hills back home, of Ma, of Tyrel and Orrin, of the Higginses, and even of the Trelawney girls.

Those Trelawney girls lived over the mountain from us, and they had the name of being a wild, harum-scarum lot, but they kept the dust rising on those mountain trails. There were eight Trelawney girls, all of them pretty, and whilst everybody else was feuding they had no feuds with anybody.

Busy as I was now a-talking, I found time to check my back trail. A man who travels wild country gets to studying where he's coming from, because some day he might have to go back, and a trail looks a lot different when you ride over it in the opposite direction.

Every tree, every mountain, has its own particular look, and each one has several appearances, so you look back over your shoulder if you want to know country. It also helps you to live a whole lot longer. Like now.

Somebody was rising a dust back there. Not a big dust . . . but a dust. It seemed to me there were four or five horses, and they were walking just to keep the dust down so as not to attract attention.

Dorinda didn't look back none at all. She was thinking, though, as I might have expected.

"It will serve him right," she said. "He tried to have you killed."

"Who?"

"Ben Mandrin. He knows you are the only one who could ride to where his gold came from. There must be a lot more of it there, or he wouldn't have wanted you dead."

139

"Could be."

"He had men waiting out in the cactus patch near the *brea* trail yesterday. They were out there all day, only you dodged them somehow."

"You got to give him credit for tryin'."

"I'd like to see his face when he finds the gold gone. It will be just what he deserves."

Now I took a careful look at her. It seemed to me she was doing a lot of thinking, and I hoped my Bible was still in my saddlebags. When I turned in tonight I wanted it under my pillow.

"There must be a lot of it," she said. "He told me about a ship he sank off the coast of Panama. It was loaded with gold from Peru. He told me how they had brought it ashore and up a canyon to the hiding place. It took them a week to get it all out of the ship and up to where they took it . . . only working at night, of course."

"Now that there," I said, "would be a lot of gold."

"When we get it," she said, "we can go to New York, Paris, London . . . everywhere. And you can buy the biggest, finest ranch you can find, and stock it with the finest horses and cattle."

"I sure could . . . if I had that much gold."

"You know where it is . . . and you have the mules to carry it away."

"That old man is crippled up. No telling what will happen in the future, and he may need that gold. If he don't, Roderigo might."

She turned in her saddle and stared at me like she figured me for crazy, and I expect she was right.

"You mean you're not going after it?"

"No, ma'am, I'm not. Maybe a few years from now when that old man is dead and gone, I'll come back and look around, and if he hasn't taken the last of it, I shall."

"Why, he tried to kill you! And after all you did for him!"

"That's his way. There's a mighty hard old man, Dorinda, a mighty hard old man. Right from the start I sort of half expected it. I don't think folks have ever been very friendly to him . . . not unless they figured to get something for it."

Her eyes got narrowed down and mean. "Do you intend that for me?"

"Not necessarily. It's just the way it's been for him. But he owes me nothing. Look at the mules he gave me."

"Mules! When you could have all that gold?"

She took off her hat then, and the next thing I knew two Winchesters were looking over a rock at me, and I heard horses coming up from behind. Dorinda's hand dropped over mine as I reach for my six-shooter.

"There you are, boys. Make him talk."

She drew away from me, taking my gun with her. I took a careful look around, but they had me. They had me dead to rights, and there just wasn't anything I could do about it.

There were six of them, and my Winchester was in the boot, and it might as well have been back in Prescott for all the good it would do me.

"Take him, boys. He's all yours." Dorinda's black eyes showed all the witch in her now. I think she was ready to shoot me herself, only they still didn't know where all that gold was.

One thing I did know. There was no way out of this one.

ten

The way I'd taken in leaving the ranch was north into the hills. It had been in my mind, for I'd still no stock of goods to sell at the Arizona mines, to cross over the mountains to San Francisco Ranch where Newhall was building a town. Folks said he already had the finest hotel south of San Francisco there, and the railroad and stage line passed through the town.

Goods were reported to be as cheap there as in Los Angeles . . . even cheaper, some said, because Fields, who ran the store, was trying to keep folks from riding all the way into Los Angeles to trade.

We'd ridden westward a ways and were just about to cut back into the hills and head north when these men moved down on me. No question but what that blackeyed girl had planned it that way. If I'd gone to where the old man had hidden his gold, these men would have followed and taken it from me. Now that I hadn't gone that way, they were going to force me to tell them where it was.

If I reached for my rifle I'd be dead before my

hand fairly grasped the action, let alone got it clear of the scabbard. Yes, they had me dead to rights.

The place they'd picked to stop me was near a big rock at one end of a small valley . . . and I had a strong hunch this was the very *potrero* that lay below the ridge where all that gold was hidden.

It was a pretty little valley, with some fine old oaks around, and we'd stopped almost in the shade of one of them. It was a still, warm afternoon, and I could hear the birds talking it up back in the trees and brush just off the trail.

They moved in around me in a narrowing circle. I let my hands rest on the pommel and tried to see my way out, but my mind was a blank.

"He took the old man out that night, boys," Dorinda said, "so he's got to know where the gold is."

"He wouldn't take me to it. Do you think he's crazy?"

Nobody said anything, and then after a bit one of them spoke up. "How about that, ma'am?"

"How far can an old man crawl? It took them time to ride out and back, so if Old Ben left him up there, he can't have gone far. There's been no rain, so we should get a few indications of direction."

The black-eyed gunman tilted his Winchester. "You going to tell us, mister? You going to take us there?"

Well, why not? It wasn't my gold, and once they had it they'd have no further use for me. They might just let me go . . . although they might figure it best to shoot me so's I couldn't come back at them.

"Far's I know, he got it all. Else do you think I'd not be up there looking?"

"If that was all there was," Dorinda said, "he'd not have cared in the least about you seeing the place. No, it took them several nights of work to take that treasure up there from the beach, so he couldn't possibly bring all of it away in one night."

"We'd have to pack grub," I said. "It's far from here, and I'm carrying nothing. I was figuring to stock up at Newhall's place."

"He's lying," Dorinda said. "I tracked them part of the way."

Now I taken another look at her. This witch woman certainly knew a sight of things no city girl should know. She had tracked us, she said, and I had a hunch she wasn't lying about that. If she had tracked us, she must be pretty good.

"It's not far from here," she said. "I tracked them for several miles in this direction, and they couldn't have ridden much further than this."

They were all around me. There was no chance to make a move without getting killed, or at least badly hurt. My mules were over there feeding on the grass along with my spare horses.

"My guess is that we aren't more than a mile or two from it right now," Dorinda said, "and if I'd not been along he'd have gone right to it."

She turned toward a tall, tough-looking blond man. "Clymer, you and the Yaqui make him talk."

The Yaqui was flat-featured, a half-breed by the look of him, and a man who would know how to make a man die slowly. The Yaquis were said to be as good at that as the Apaches.

If I tried a run for it, there was no shelter close by. The trees were too scattered, and that big rock was almost sheer.

Time and again I'd been in tight spots, and somehow I'd come out of them, and it seemed as if this here one ought to be so easy. It was such a pleasant day, the sun made leaf shadows on the ground around, and a few high, lazy clouds drifted in the sky. There was no violence around . . . except in that ring of silent guns, aimed at me.

It shouldn't happen like this, I told myself. This is all wrong. There should be shouts and guns exploding, and fighting; there should be blood and the smell of gunpowder.

There were none of those things, and here I was, flat against a wall, with no way out.

"Get down off that horse," Clymer said. He was grinning at me, and I saw he was missing two teeth. "We're going to see what kind of stuff you got in you."

He gestured toward the Yaqui. "I seen him skin a man alive one time . . . well, almost. That feller got smart and done what we told him. Not soon enough, though, because when we let him be it was already too late."

There was a moment there when I thought about jabbing a spur into the stallion and taking my chances, but the trouble was, there wasn't any chance. Those guns just couldn't miss. Not all of them.

So I swung down, and they walked me toward a big old oak. Believe me, I was sweating. I was scared, but I was determined not to show it, and I was watching every second for the break I hoped would come. Only it didn't come.

They walked me up to that tree, and suddenly I made up my mind. If they were going to kill me they might as well get it done. One thing I knew. Nobody was going to tie me up to a tree. Not unless I was dead or unconscious.

So I made ready. If I turned fast I might lay a hand on one of those rifles, and if I had one of those I'd take somebody with me when I passed in my checks.

"Hey," somebody said. "Who's that?"

A rider was coming along the road, coming slow and easy. He was a tall man who rode well up in the saddle, and he came riding straight on.

"Hell," one of the men said, "it's Nolan Sackett!"

"Get on with it," Dorinda said irritably. "This is no affair of his."

He rode right on up to us, and despite what Dorinda had said, nobody did anything but watch him come, including me.

"Howdy, boys!" His eyes had plenty of time to take in the situation. "If you're after that gold I figure I should be in for a share."

"You're in for nothing!" Dorinda said angrily. "Get on with it, Clymer!"

Nolan, he looked over at me and grinned, and then he taken a pistol from under his coat and tossed it to me.

It was as simple as that.

He just flicked that pistol over and I reached up and snared it, and then we stood there with two guns on them, his and mine.

It caught them flat-footed and off guard. They just didn't expect anything like that, for Nolan was one of them. The trouble was, he was also a Sackett, and blood runs thicker than branch water.

Dorinda didn't cut up and scream like some women might, although she was mad enough to fight a cougar. She just looked at him and then at me.

"You boys mount up and ride," Nolan told them. "This here's a cousin of mine, or some sort of kin, and whilst I might have let you shoot him, I don't cotton to seeing that Yaqui skin no Sackett out of his hide. You boys just ride out of here and count it time well spent."

"What if we don't?" Clymer asked belligerently.

"Well," I said, "you outnumber us, but by the time we get through shootin' a whole lot of you are

147

going to be dead, and us, too, so what will you be fighting for?"

"The hell with it," one man said, and turned his horse; and after that they just drifted away, leaving us there with Dorinda Robiseau.

"Nolan," I said. "I've got it in mind to buy goods over at Newhall's place and pack them across the Mojave to the Arizona mines. That's a lot of mules for one man."

"You got you a partner," he said.

He looked over at Dorinda. "You want to come with us, Abigail?"

"I'll see you in hell first," she said, and turning her horse, she rode off.

That was no way for a lady to talk.

A few miles down the trail I said to Nolan, "You called her Abigail."

"Sure . . . didn't you know? She's one of those no-account Trelawney girls from back yonder in the hills."

Well, I'd be damned! So that was Abigail Trelawney. But it was kind of dark back of the schoolhouse that night, and I never could tell those Trelawney girls apart.

author's note

As in all my previous books, the place names are those of actual places that existed as described at the time the story took place. Although a writer of fiction is under no compulsion to be as exact as I have chosen to be as to locale, I regard each of my novels as, in a sense, historical. Each water hole or spring, each valley, canyon, creek or mountain, each store, gambling house, or hotel exists now or did exist at the time.

The tanks visited by Sackett after leaving Dorinda are the White Tanks, and the well he next visited was Lost Horse Well, both of which are now within the limits of Joshua National Monument. The Hidden Valley where Sackett was loaned a horse is now visited by thousands of tourists, and they enter by crawling, as he did. The Button brothers actually used the valley to hide stolen horses (nobody yet knows how the horses were taken in or out), and they were killed, sometime later, in a gun battle in San Bernardino.

The house of Greek George was located near the intersection of Fountain Avenue and King's Road, only a block off the famous Sunset Strip in what is now Hollywood.

The local round-ups, called rodeos in California, were held in an area roughly between La Cienaga and Robertson streets, give or take a few blocks.

Although California is not usually considered a western state in the "wild west" conception of the term, few states were more so. Only Texas could have had more cattle, and without doubt the greatest of all ropers, as well as some of the finest horsemen, were the early Spanish-Californian vaqueros . . . roping grizzlies was a favorite sport.

By 1893 El Tejon Ranch, still one of the largest in the United States, was running more than 125,000 head of sheep and 25,000 head of cattle. Without doubt one of the greatest stock drives in western history was the movement, over uncharted trails, of 17,000 head of sheep from El Tejon Ranch to Montana in 1879, by Jose Jesus Lopez. This ranch is in the Tehachapis, only a few miles from the outskirts of Los Angeles.

No cattle baron ruled his empire with a harsher hand than did the "Big Basque" Leonis, of Calabasas; and the gun battles between Carlisle and the Kings, or that between Jim McKinney and a sheriff's posse were the equal of the OK Corral fight or any of the famous gun battles of the West. McKinney, a notorious outlaw with a number of killings behind him, shot it out in Bakersfield with Will and Burt Tibbett and Jeff Packard . . . McKinney was killed, as were Jeff Packard and Will Tibbett (the father of singer Lawrence Tibbett), Burt Tibbet killing McKinney. There was considerable testimony to the effect that Al Hulse, and perhaps another man, were also shooting at the deputies from the room where McKinney was killed.

It is an ironic fact that it was in the City of the Angels that the street called the Calle de los Negros held a record for violence and killing unequaled in the West.

ABOUT LOUIS L'AMOUR

"I think of myself in the oral tradition—as a troubador, a village taleteller, the man in the shadows of the campfire. That's the way I'd like to be remembered—as a storyteller. A good storyteller."

It is doubtful that any author could be as at home in the world re-created in his novels as Louis Dearborn L'Amour. Not only could he physically fill the boots of the rugged characters he writes about, but he literally has "walked the land my characters walk." His personal experiences as well as his lifelong devotion to historical research have combined to give Mr. L'Amour the unique knowledge and understanding of the people, events, and challenge of the American frontier which have become the hallmarks of his popularity.

Of French-Irish descent, Mr. L'Amour can trace his own family in North America back to the early 1600s and follow their steady progression westward, "always on the frontier." As a boy growing up in Jamestown, North Dakota, he absorbed all he could about his family's frontier heritage, including the story of his great-grandfather who was scalped by Sioux warriors.

Spurred by an eager curiosity and desire to broaden his horizons, Mr. L'Amour left home at the age of fifteen and enjoyed a wide variety of jobs including seaman, lumberjack, elephant handler, skinner of dead cattle, assessment miner, and officer on tank destroyers during World War II. During his "yondering days" he also circled the world on a freighter, sailed a dhow on the Red Sea, was shipwrecked in the West Indies and stranded in the Mojave Desert. He has won fifty-one of fifty-nine fights as a professional boxer and worked as a journalist and lecturer. A voracious reader and collector of rare books, Mr. L'Amour's personal library of some 10,000 volumes covers a broad range of scholarly disciplines including many personal papers, maps, and diaries of the pioneers.

Mr. L'Amour "wanted to write almost from the time I could walk." After developing a widespread following for his many adventure stories written for the fiction magazines, Mr. L'Amour published his first full-length novel, *Hondo*, in 1953. Mr. L'Amour is now one of the four bestselling living novelists in the world. Every one of his more than 85 novels is constantly in print and every one has sold more than one million copies, giving him more million-copy bestsellers than any other living author. His books have been translated into more than a dozen languages, and more than thirty of his novels and stories have been made into feature films and television movies.

The recipient of many great honors and awards, Mr. L'Amour in 1983 became the first novelist ever to be awarded a Special National Gold Medal by the United States Congress in honor of his life's work. In 1984 he was also awarded the Medal of Freedom by President Ronald Reagan.

Mr. L'Amour lives in Los Angeles with his wife, Kathy, and their two children, Beau and Angelique.